I DON'T WANT TO HURT YOU

Miktos Press

I DON'T WANT TO HURT YOU

A Thriller

Benjamin Lampkin

To M, my support

To Ell, my boogie

To Evie, my biddie

"All I Really Need,
Is to Know That You Believe."

P. R. Nelson

Table of Contents

Prologue

The cold felt wrong. It made no sense to Jessie Schuetter. Not then, not at that time of year, not ever, really, in that part of Indiana. The crackling of the freshly formed ice on the nearby pond was wrong, she knew it as she tied her hair in long brown braids and put in her contacts in the darkness of the abbreviated galley kitchen. She knew the sun would be wrong when it slowly ascended through the bare maple trees and walnuts and elms that covered the leaf-strewn slopes along the sides of the road. Her clothes felt wrong, especially the stiff jeans rubbing the bare skin underneath, her pale white skin that had always looked wrong and felt wrong, except next to Tyner's.

The tree provided some privacy, a spot where no one could see him. Snow piled around his feet, began to build on his head in uneven patches, numbed the ends of his fingers and the tips of his ears, but he pretended not to notice. He'd been there many times, watching, waiting for a sign, but it looked different through the downfall of white flakes. A head appeared in the window, lit from behind by the soft glow of a quiet little table lamp, and he marveled, as always, at her beauty, at the eyes that seemed almost swollen with feeling. She stared outside, she couldn't see him, he knew she couldn't, but he knew she felt him there. No matter what, no matter the time, when he arrived, when he took up his place and looked in at her, she looked out.

He watched her step outside, open the door to the van and start the engine. He watched the sulfurous clouds drifting away from the muffler, illuminated by the bright rear lights and a flickering bulb atop a pole leaning casually near the driveway. He watched her walk outside, a small child in each arm, another walking wordlessly next to her. He watched her drive away.

Muted sniffles sounded from the back of the van. The oldest, Jazmin, cradled her favorite stuffie, a mangled looking giraffe that had ceased resembling any earthly creature. Jett slept soundly in her pink snowsuit. Occasional cries of hunger and little whimpers from the baby, Georgy, she ignored it all and kept driving. No other cars on Staufenberger Road, no early risers commuting across the river or down the hill, no farmers that she could see trundling a round bale to a herd of cattle out in a blackened pasture.

"Momma," Jazmin said softly, her voice partially muffled by the giraffe blocking her mouth. "Where are we going?"

"Don't worry, baby." She kept her eyes locked on the dark roads, the trees looming overhead. The snow fell heavier and faster, her windshield wipers had trouble keeping up and she increased the intensity, slowed the van to under 30 mph as she neared a curve in the road. It wasn't what she expected, or wanted, the freezing temps, the foggy exhalations, the stiff hands, the nearly silent children. She was too cold, but she had no choice. Kept moving. It was time. The day had arrived, and she was ready, and the kids were ready. The wheels crunched over hardened gravel as she turned the van onto a little access road just past the curve. She'd seen it before and knew where it led. To salvation. To redemption. To the end.

He watched her turn. He followed.

Chapter 1

Blake Prince opened his eyes slightly, the glare coming in hard through the window and forcing him to pull the thin sheet over his eyes. He shivered, hunted with a free arm for the blanket that always seemed to slide off in the night. Pain rippled through his head, waves of sharp stabs that forced him to get up and seek a glass of water and aspirin. A beep from the phone, an insignificant notification, probably, or another bit of bad news that he couldn't do a thing about, he ignored it and looked for a clean cup or glass, couldn't find one, dumped out some brackish liquid from a souvenir Cincinnati Reds cup and filled it with tap water, swallowed half, chucked some pills in his mouth, swallowed the rest.

It had been another long night. One of many from the past couple of years. Started with a bourbon and Coke, then a handful of beers, then shots of tequila, then more beers. Somehow he made it home, he was glad he lived so close to his favorite spot and didn't need to drive, but he couldn't say whether someone had dropped him off or he'd walked the mile by himself. Nothing registered in his memory. Didn't really matter, he'd done the walk enough, as long as he was upright and the ground was dry and traffic was light, he could make it.

He debated returning to bed, looked at the clock on the microwave and saw that it was already 10:30. Looked closer, saw his eyes in the glass' reflection, lifeless brown, like a rotting log resting on the banks of a creek perpetually worn down by wind, water, sun, time. A shower would help, more water, some food, but that all felt like so much effort. He ignored the thumping in his head, trudged to the bathroom, the door only steps from the kitchen, and peeled off his shirt and boxers, the stench of stale beer permeating the fabric and curling his nose. The hot water poured down, he stood almost motionless for 10 minutes and let the spray cover him, drench his hair that he'd grown out into a slight curl, pool at his feet, until the liquid faded to lukewarm, then cool, and he smothered his hair and face and body in soap and rinsed and leapt out, his only towel smelled of mildew and lay crumpled by the toilet but he had no choice and dried off quickly with it. A swipe across the mirror revealed most of his face, and he studied the scruff on his chin and cheeks, the color still slightly red, just like his hair, and bailed on a shave after taking a glance at his crusty razor.

Outside, a howl of wind attacked as he hunted for clean clothes in the main room of the apartment, the windows shimmied and the door rattled and the garage doors below seemed to crumple and crackle against the gale. Then quiet, an odd quiet, as his apartment sat near Central Avenue, which fed cars in and out of downtown almost all day, but there was nothing, and he flipped on the TV for something to fill the space, made a bowl of cereal and grabbed the half bottle of Gatorade left in the fridge, sat down at the little table, and opened his laptop to prepare for work.

They didn't really know him or what he was like, his editors at the online magazine, Analectic News, but he turned in clean copy, on time every time, and so they continued to give him assignments. He usually turned in two or three a week and cleared $250 per article, enough to cover his rent and utilities and car insurance, but he'd also gone a week or sometimes two with nothing to do and no extra cash, so he'd resorted to picking up shifts here and there at the Fulfillment Warehouse across the river just to have enough to go out.

He ate his cereal slowly and scanned his email, no assignment but the promise of one soon, and he frowned in disappointment. I should have checked first before going to all the trouble of waking myself up with a pointless shower, he thought. Another beep from his phone, it was lost somewhere in the sheets and he didn't feel like retrieving it, the phone was not an appendage to him, just a tool, so he ignored the pestering sounds and lights whenever he wanted. Considered going for a run, he enjoyed the heavy breathing and dense feeling in his chest and the rubbery legs, and often pushed himself longer and harder the day after putting away too many drinks.

The pull of the Internet, though. He started chatting with a friend, a seamless exchange of gibberish with a guy he hadn't seen face to face in more than two years. Flipped over to YouTube and left multiple comments on multiple videos. Tapped out a few random Tweets about the deluge of snow pouring down on Troy City and his inability to muster the enthusiasm to work a shift at the warehouse. There were a few time slots available, he could have gone from 1 to 4, or 2 to 5, even 2 to 7 if he wanted more hours, but he clicked out of the sign-in page and returned to wasting time. A circular DVD holder stood by the TV and he went over, spun it a couple of times, looking for something to watch, something he'd seen a dozen times and knew by heart but still delighted him.

Movies, good movies, that was his thing, everyone who knew him expected a barrage of quotes and exaggerated facial expressions tied to his favorite characters. He championed classics and foreign movies his friends had never heard of, and looked down on anyone who loved big, stupid blockbusters and romances and comic-book movies. The cold weather made him long for something exciting, and he pulled out a copy of *The Killer*, and marvelled at the relentless action and ceaseless gunfire and Chow-Yun Fat's meticulous hair.

He quickly checked his phone, no missed calls, no voice mails, and he tossed it aside. He opened another browser, went to his blog, and started typing, one sentence at a time, one paragraph after another, he typically wrote posts about the movies he'd just watched, and spent nearly an hour poring over the meaning of the doves and the church in the climactic battle scene. He hadn't been inside a church in half a decade, not since that night, he thought, the night everything changed.

A message, the name familiar, it was one he'd chosen, Clarke, from *Mo Betta' Blues*, he thought it was a great name but she didn't seem to care one way or another. As long as no one found out it was really her. I promise, he told her, and though he'd hinted to some friends about something going on with a slightly older woman, he'd kept all the details hidden, kept his promise.

Need to see you soon, Clarke wrote, he always read the messages from her as if that was her real name, it was a game he liked to play, to pretend she was really his. Park in the same spot, meet me in the place at 9:30. He wrote back immediately, *Ok.* That was all he needed to say.

The rest of the day tumbled slowly by in a haze of half-naps, snacks, a few pulls off his disposable pen, and a dogged pursuit of an auction on eBay for a vintage copy of Shuggie Otis' *Freedom Flight* on vinyl. He lost, secretly a little happy that he hadn't spent another $40 on a record, then got dressed, pulled a cleanish pair of jeans on, a v-neck undershirt, thin purple sweater, Original Penguin sneakers, and his long black coat. Debated walking or driving to Schwarz's but decided on driving, he'd only have one drink there, just a beer, before he went over to Clarke's.

Blake bounded through the yard, careful not to slip on the snow, his shoes not built for the weather or the amount of running he had to do to reach the little building. Her instructions never wavered: drive the long route, around Red Creek and Marshall Road, up Little Stone Way, pull into the abandoned gravel road down the road, walk on the asphalt until you reach the yard, step through the grass and navigate around the trees, stop at the last one, wait until the light comes on, then run to the door and enter without making a sound. Tyner, his oldest friend, taught him about women, how to approach them, how to stand with quiet strength and confidence, how to listen and say just a few words to win them over. So when Blake met Clarke, he followed Tyner's advice, let her talk, smiled and tilted his head and looked as seductive as possible and nonchalantly asked her if it'd be cool to give her a call sometime. She said yes, of course, and before long she unveiled the rules to him.

She stood in front of a bar cart opposite the door, poured red wine into a bulbous glass, didn't turn around at the feel of cold air rushing around her bare legs, the color of her skin so much paler in the bleakness of the winter. The room looked like a weird combination of a hunting cabin and wine bar, pictures of deer and ducks and beavers hung on the walls in random positions, along with vintage posters and artwork of bottles of cabernet and beaujolais and strange Italian apertifs. A massive couch dominated the space, with high armrests covered in gold fringe and a hefty mink blanket hugging the back. No TV, no stereo, just stacks of old books on little tables and various stands, and a non-working fireplace fitted with a grate stacked with tall white candles emitting their eerie yellow glow. Two doors opened off the kitchenette, one to the bedroom, one to a small bathroom. So many little changes from the first time he was there, more wine bottles festooned with French and Italian names, all the mirrors removed, all traces of children wiped out, all the shades perpetually drawn. The iconography remained, a large wooden crucifix nailed to one wall, a picture of a bearded and melancholy Jesus in a frame, Blake did his best to ignore them, but remembered Clarke stopping one time, very early on, right in the middle of things, lifted the sheet to her chin, and told him, "We have to stop. He's watching." Panicked, Blake delicately lifted the corner of the curtain, but she stopped him. "No. Jesus is watching." He left, presumably never to return, but she contacted him less than a week later, neither speaking of the incident nor of Jesus.

She took her wine glass into the bedroom, never turned around to look at Blake, her hair so penetrating in its acute blackness. He knew there were people in the mansion just 50 yards away, a husband, a kid or two, but he never asked questions, he never searched online, and never heard a thing from her. He followed, into the dark, and saw her on the bed.

There was a possibility he could be seen, a small one, but he'd parked far enough away, he believed. Besides, she was too focused on the kids, keeping the older ones from straying from her sight, keeping them upright and moving through the heavy snow. They walked for a couple of minutes, their voices and footsteps muffled, Jessie doing her best to reassure them that everything would be all right as they trudged deeper into the woods.

So far, so good. She was making her way to the spot, no one was around, the light had faded to almost nothing, and he could see everything from his almost abstract point of view. He knew what she'd been thinking when she left the little house with the kids, knew she was expecting a little piece of herself to be born again. But she wasn't expecting him.

Chapter 2

Blake knew he'd lucked into the enviable position of having a woman request his presence at random times, with the sole purpose being an exchange of pleasure. No, Clarke was not a side piece, he'd tried calling her that when he texted with his friend Les and immediately felt bad, plus it wasn't entirely accurate. You have to have a main piece in order to have a side piece, and Clarke was the only woman in Blake's life. Technically, Blake could be considered her side piece, but he did his best not to let that enter into his mind.

The two met years earlier, when Blake's career prospects loomed over conversations and relationships and he knew how to let people know he'd soon be a big deal. She spotted him from a distance, across the banquet hall, through the twinkling Christmas lights and the decorations, they were at a holiday charity event that required $500 per plate, but Blake had been invited by a mentor, and Clarke was on the arm of her soon-to-be husband. Their conversation lasted briefly, an introduction and exchange of names and a quick sizing up, and they parted, didn't see or speak to each other for years, though he remembered her big eyes and stunning physical beauty. But he returned to Troy City, and she found out, and she set their current agreement in motion with a series of benign messages that morphed into flirting and a secret invitation.

The snow had let up by the time he got back to his Camry, and brilliant shafts of moonlight let him pull out of the gravel drive and away from Clark's place without having to turn on the headlights. Another of Clarke's rules, make sure no one sees you, even if you have to drive in the dark, but one he had to violate on supremely black nights. He listened to the classic rock station for a few minutes, switched to R&B but frowned upon hearing a skittering, trap-based track that was decidedly not old school. Why do they insist on ruining this station, he thought, just stick to the good stuff, none of this watered-down crap will ever top Marvin or Stevie or Luther or Patrice. He wondered why his tastes hadn't evolved, why he could not find anything to satisfy his extremely discerning ear, but dismissed the thought as another sampled hi-hat roll dinged out of the speakers. He got home and pulled another couple of drags, the battery holding up much longer than he'd expected, and fell asleep to the sounds of "I'd Rather Be With You" and Bootsy's whimsical vocals.

A heavy pounding snapped him out of bed, he rubbed his eyes and waited, heard the sound again, pushed out of bed and opened the flimsy fiberglass door separating his apartment from the stairs leading down to the garage and workshop. No one there, he just saw his dad's old Thunderbird and some lawn mowing equipment and a collection of tools that had been slowly oxidizing for years, so he gripped the handrail and walked gingerly to the concrete floor, crossed over to a heavier, bolted door on the side of the workshop.

"Mom. Hey, good morning." He wiped his face and ran his hands through his hair, but he knew he looked like a mess, his t-shirt wrinkled, his long briefs bunched around his thighs. Despite working part-time and living above the garage, he didn't want to disappoint his mother by looking slovenly on the rare occasions he saw her, but he didn't feel like bothering with clothes or showering even though it was almost lunchtime.

"Blake, I've been calling you," she said, her hands clasped, her face heavy and somber, her thin shoulders shaking beneath a black sweater. The wind had died down but still whipped around and tossed her long hair still streaked with blonde and disentangled pockets of snow from the ground and sent flurries everywhere. "What have you heard? Do you know anything?"

"What do you mean? What are you talking about?"

"Your friend, Tyner. They found his wife, Jessie and the kids. They're dead. They're all dead."

Blake didn't move, didn't speak, his hand nearly frozen to the door handle, his eyes unblinking as he stared at his mother. Everyone knew Tyner Hayes, everyone in Troy City, everyone in Hudson County. Little old ladies. Doctors and lawyers. Warehouse workers. Business owners from up and down the economic spectrum. A Southern Indiana basketball legend, definitely, if not an icon throughout the state. Tyner drew people in, not only with his game and his on-court style but his megawatt smile, flashed at any and everyone in town and at the press, and his chocolate skin and engulfing hands and confident, lanky stroll, he had a presence, he seemed taller than his 6 feet 5 inches, his clothes seemed cooler than their price tag, his spiky, twisted hair was replicated by all the little boys in town, even the little Caucasian kids, and mothers and fathers had no problems if he showed up to pick up their daughter for a date. Fans packed the gym at Troy City High School and at high schools throughout the region, waited hours for tickets, stood shoulder to shoulder in the rafters to watch him play. Adults lined up with their kids for autographs after games, shouted his name as he walked through the grocery store, pestered him with questions about where he would go to college, usually pleading with him to become a Hoosier. When he broke the school scoring record as a junior, students tossed homemade confetti on the court. When he led Troy City to a regional title, local artists painted his face and jersey number on the sides of buildings all over town.

When he became an All-American, city leaders put up a sign outside the city that read "Welcome to Troy City, Home of Tyner Hayes." When the Bluebirds won the state title his senior year, his teammates carried him off the court on their shoulders, and the mayor authorized the city council to organize a massive parade that drew thousands of fans to downtown Troy on a cold, rainy Wednesday afternoon. When he chose to attend college at Temple University, the announcement made the front page of the local paper and was the biggest sports story of the day, even 25 minutes away over in Louisville.

Blake and Tyner grew up together, went to the same elementary school, played baseball and football and basketball on the same teams, ran through the neighborhood at night knocking on doors and agitating dogs, calling girls in middle school and leaving obnoxious but sincere messages. When Tyner became a star, Blake was there, writing stories for the school paper and uploading videos of him dunking on little white boys. When Tyner needed help getting a car, Blake asked his dad for help, and they found a Buick that an old lady was willing to part with for $500. When one of his girlfriends got pregnant, Blake drove her to a clinic in Indianapolis and kept his mouth shut. When he needed a ride home from Philadelphia after failing to secure an agent and not getting drafted and not getting invited to any pro team workouts, Blake left school early and missed a final to bring him back to Indiana.

"When did you hear this?" Blake asked, suddenly aware of the cold and his lack of clothing, and he reached for his mom's arm and ushered her into the garage.

"Earlier, I texted you a bunch and you didn't answer."

"Yeah, I know, I was tired, I've been working on some stuff."

"God, it's just so awful, I can't believe what happened."

"Is he alive? Is he in jail? What the hell's going on?"

"Blake, no one knows where he is. Please, can you do something?" He took a moment, still shivering, and looked at his mom. She looked so frightened, so unsure of what to do, and he felt like grabbing her, but instead she lunged at him and wrapped her arms around his neck, squeezed, and held on. Our first hug in three years, he thought. Because of this.

"Listen, mom, I'll try and find out what's going on and let you know. Go call Landa and ask her if she knows anything."

"I did, but I'll ask again. Are you working later?" He shook his head, and she turned and shuffled back into the cold and the snow, her feet crunching on powder and a thin sheet of ice that wasn't there the night before. He watched her for a second, watched her carefully step across the covered sidewalk and the stairs that led into the back room off the kitchen. He'd walked through that door so many times, usually leaping up and over the bottom steps and nearly crashing into the glass before yanking it open and tearing inside, in search of food, or a cold drink, or someone to talk to about his latest adventure with Tyner or Les Stephens or Jeff Allen, his boys. They were all off in another place now, except Jamie and Tyner, both in Troy City, both disappointments, on some level, and neither ready to give in and make a call and become real friends again.

Back upstairs, he scoured all the sites, the local paper and the Louisville stations and the ex-journalists and current bloggers and anyone with even the slightest connection to Tyner and Jessie. The same headline, just rearranged, shouted at him on every page: "Bodies of missing family found near creek, officials say." He couldn't stop, he read everything, every story, the poorly constructed blog posts and the sloppily-worded excerpts from on-air stories. He refreshed his email every few minutes, looked through every social media account, tried to find some mention of Tyner, other than his three kids and girlfriend being the victim of a crime no one was sure what to make of.

"Local investigators remain puzzled about the discovery of four bodies, including three children, near Birdseye Creek in rural Hudson County. Jessie Schuetter, 26, was found beside her children just after 8 a.m. by a passing motorist, who noticed Schuetter's silver van parked along an abandoned road less than a mile from St. Aureus Church in Iona. All four bodies were found in the snow but there were no immediate signs of foul play. The family was reported missing after the children did not report to school or daycare and Schuetter did not show up for work. Police are asking for anyone with knowledge of the family's previous whereabouts to contact them with any information. Schuetter is believed to be the girlfriend of former All-American Tyner Hayes, 27, who is the father of the three children."

It took him a while to regain his composure, to come to terms with what he'd read, what was true. The little kids, all three, were gone. Jessie, gone. Dead in the cold and the snow in a random field. All he could do, all he could muster, was a scant message on social media, spread across his many accounts, that read simply, "Sending my condolences to Tyner, you'll always be family. We'll get through this."

He tried to find more details but every story repeated the same scant details, and reiterated the slightly unconfirmed relationship between Jessie and Tyner. Blake knew better, that they were likely no longer together, but he hadn't exactly heard the story from Tyner himself. They hadn't spoken in over a year, other than a congratulatory text Blake sent after the birth of the youngest kid.

Les let him know that Jessie had moved out, taken the kids to live in a small house about 15 miles away, and Tyner wasn't happy about it.

Blake hesitated. I should reach out, he thought, and truly give Tyner my condolences, ask him if there's anything I can do. But it could easily be construed as insincere, he had expressed his displeasure over their relationship ever since he met Jessie over summer break before their senior years in college. She lived in Hudson County but wasn't from Troy City, her family came from one of the small blips on the map way out in the hills that hovered over the rest of the county, a place that Blake had never been to. A pretty girl, certainly, with long, slender legs and sumptuous dark hair and green eyes, but Blake worried instantly about the two of them together, their repartee so schmaltzy and their PDA so graphic that he found it annoying to be around them for more than a few minutes. But it was also Jessie's relentless pursuit of trying to remake him, to turn him into something Blake knew he wasn't. She invoked lots of homespun, intimate tales of their future together, a home and kids and a gentle life in the country with no worries. And Blake knew that wasn't what Tyner wanted, the glamour of being a pro ball player had been his dream since they were kids, and to hear him soberly agree with Jessie about eventually moving back to Troy City infuriated him.

So he started putting her down, called her a gold digger, white trash, a loser who'd never leave the county and never be anything. Well, no, he never went that far, they were friends but even he knew he wasn't above an ass-whooping for talking shit about Tyner's girl. He wanted to say all those things, he never did, but his attitude came across in other ways, how he ignored her, and never sat or stood near her, and let slip some biting comments every now and then. About the benefits of community college to a person like her, about Tyner moving to a big city and being rich, about all the crazy adventures and experiences he was going to have. Not so subtle digs, and an obvious ploy to plant doubt in Tyner's mind.

There was also her family. Blake never knew how many of them there truly were, the whole family tree seemed to be comprised of bands of religious weirdos who holed up in Bochim in some kind of self-contained compound, farmed for themselves and fortified their acreage with barb-wire fencing and tall, padlocked gates and heavy rows of pine trees that obscured views for anyone trying to get a peek at the homes and the people who lived and worked and worshipped out there. Blake had heard the stories, of apocalyptic preaching and men and women writhing on the ground at church services, gibberish spewing from their mouths, white cloths covering prone parishioners, kids running around with their hands in the air and eyes rolled back in their heads, a bearded pastor opening his mouth wide and pointing to his gold tooth as proof of his special relationship with God. He'd heard of bunkers built into sandstone hills, with heavy metal doors that were impossible to pry open, and semi trailers loaded with water pumped from underground springs, women with long, braided hair tending gardens, young men driving tractors over green knobs of farmland, teenagers feeding chickens and goats and horses, smaller kids with dirt-smeared faces teetering around a small building and playing with homemade toys while a handful of older ladies looked on. The men operated a lumber mill and made furniture to keep the community afloat, though some worked other jobs outside the village as laborers and construction workers. Some families sent their kids to outside schools, and some teenagers left and never returned. Rumors swirled about arranged marriages and some kind of prophet who ran the whole commune from one of the bunkers, but no one outside of Bochim had seen or heard him for decades.

Darker stories emerged over the years. Of bizarre, almost pagan rituals conducted at night around large bonfires, and girls forced into sexual relationships with older men, and medieval punishments administered to unbelievers and usurpers. All tales that had never been proven, but a body was found in Bochim in the 1980s, a man in his early 20s with a thick mustache and a lean torso who'd come to the place on his own just a year earlier. The sheriff's office became involved after he'd been missing for more than two weeks, all the people in the community affirming that they had not suspected anything and assumed he'd simply taken off to live elsewhere. The county went through the 2,000 acres with dogs and a search and rescue team, traversing the thick forests and rocky ravines on foot and using one of the family's boats to search the lake. One of the dogs pulled out a scrap of muddy blue jean material from a swampy runoff next to the lake, and within minutes they'd found the body, the forehead scraped from long shards of creekstone, the hands wrinkled, sheafs of skin sloughed off, the fingernails black, mud and dirt packed unevenly onto the body. No suspects ever emerged in the man's death, no one ever knew what happened or why he ended up face down in that part of the lake, and eventually authorities had to conclude that his death was an accident.

Somehow, Jessie came out of that odd little place, which was hunkered down between the ridges of northern Hudson County all on its own. She went to public school, dated, drove a car, and met Tyner while she worked part-time at an optometrist's office. Before his senior year at Temple came to an end, he told Blake that Jessie was pregnant, and that no matter what he'd take care of her.

He worked out with a handful of players from Philadelphia at an open gym in the hopes of securing interest from an agent or a scout or general manager, but nothing came of it. Reporters questioned him about his next moves and he told them all he'd return to Troy City to regroup, to continue working on his game and try and get a shot at playing in one of the minor leagues or possibly moving to Europe. He played briefly in Puerto Rico, then in Venezuala, but otherwise he never left. He had a degree from Temple, majored in business management, and the combination of a legitimate, completed education and his star power earned him plenty of interviews with managers and executives and city leaders. A transportation supply company made him the best offer, gave him the highest salary and a manager's title, and he took it, moved into an apartment with Jessie, volunteered as a coach at Fifer Middle School, and ran a summer basketball camp that drew over a hundred kids.

They stayed kind of close, but Tyner was pulled in too many directions, Blake left for medical school in Ohio, and so began the gradual disintegration of their friendship. No more phone calls, no more emails, not that there were ever many of those, and very rarely did they see each other in person. A text-based relationship, one that consisted of little jokes and simple greetings and promises to get together at vague points in the future. Sometimes those promises came to fruition, and Blake would show up to the

Mill or Schwarz's and down a beer with Tyner, the whole time mesmerized by the cavalcade of fans who stopped to shake his hand or pat his shoulder or wish him well or regale him with a story of some game or play or shot that became lodged in their consciousness forever. They all got a handshake and a deep, mirthful look in the eyes, but Blake always noticed when Tyner turned back around the shroud of disappointment that spread across his face, knowing he was sitting in a bar in Troy and not in some fancy club in Miami or L.A., or even Madrid or Berlin. He'd be going home to Jessie, and their apartment, and their kids.

A low gurgling popped up from the kitchen, Blake jerked a little, forgetting about the pod of Vienna Roast he'd popped into the coffee maker when he got up the steps. The coffee masked the other aromas in the room, the musty carpet that needed to be vacuumed, unwashed dishes in the sink and on the counter, the sweet, woody cologne he'd waded through the night before and dotted all the other surfaces and created a sickeningly thin but intrusive dusting of musk. He walked to the kitchenette and poured four packets of sweetener into the coffee, looked up at the photo of his grandparents atop a cabinet, his grandmother dark and regal, his grandfather light and flashing a gold-toothed smile, who would have scoffed at his sugary coffee and shook their heads in pure disappointment and disapproval at his life. Grandpa used to run his town's sewage and water plants and farmed several plots of land in their little county in central Illinois, and Grandma had operated a salon out of her house since the early 70s. He was not what they intended.

The street noise rose up through the poorly ventilated windows and Blake stood with his coffee, watched the electric and telephone wires swaying as they dipped from pole to pole. He imagined the bodies out in the snow, Jazmin clinging to Jett as protectively as possible, Jessie with her arms wrapped around the baby and her head ducked down to provide as much warmth as she could. His phone rang and he made a move toward it, his heart suddenly racing at the thought of hearing more bad news. Or hearing from Tyner.

"Hello? No, Landa, I haven't," he said, letting his sister know he still hadn't reached out to Tyner. "Yeah, I'll check right now." They each hung up, so familiar with the other's bluntness that little formalities didn't matter, they left without saying goodbye, ignored calls and texts without worrying about the other getting upset, never hugged or said I love you. And never exchanged a true cross word.

Refreshing the web site took a few seconds, and when it all emerged he almost dropped his coffee. Tyner's face displayed prominently at the top. And the word suspect.

Chapter 3

"Please, can you tell me something?" Blake felt the phone crushing his ear but ignored the pain, waited for a few seconds to hear a word from the other side.

"I don't know any more than you do, Blake. He isn't allowed to give me details."

"Bullshit, I know he tells you things when he wants to. I gotta know more than what they're putting out there."

"Listen, Blake," his sister said, her voice way calmer than his, any moment she was likely to tell him to shut the hell up and hang up. "Amos is a cop, he's just one cop, he doesn't always know everything. And he won't risk getting in trouble, not for you."

The quiet standoff continued for a few more seconds, their breathing heavy and slightly labored. "He didn't do it. Tell me they don't think he really did it."

"I don't know what they think." The website reloaded again, this time a picture of Tyner from his senior year, the year he cemented his status in Hudson County and throughout Indiana, holding the state champion trophy in one hand and a piece of the snipped net in the other, his smile enormous but his eyes lacking any real joy, the moment just another in a long line of celebration and worship he'd been a part of for four years.

He hung up, wondering what to do, who to talk to. Tyner's family wouldn't be of any help or use, his mom had aged and withered past the point of being anything more than a worried soul, his dad lived out of state, his sister lived in Seattle. He texted the guys a link to the story and asked them if they had spoken to Tyner recently, if they knew what he'd been up to or knew what was going on between him and Jessie. Nothing out of the ordinary, they both said, he'd been working the same hours and organizing his camp and seeing the kids, and he and Jessie were on another break. A common relationship tactic for the two of them, Blake had housed Tyner once before when he and Jessie split briefly, not long after Jazmin was born, but they always returned to each other, Tyner never wanting to be away from his kids for too long, and Jessie not wanting to be away from him. She was more than a girlfriend, more than a devoted partner, she had latched onto to his persona almost instantly and never wavered in her undying devotion to him, but she couldn't contain such feelings, her love frequently breached and spilled over into explosions of jealousy and rage that consumed their entire family and forced him to flee.

Sometimes she left, stuffed clothes in a handful of suitcases and filled a box with toys and took the kids and the minivan. There was always a place for her in Bochim, a basement or spare room or even an entire floor she could occupy for a few days or weeks until things smoothed over. But a dispute erupted the last time she stayed there, one of her brothers and his wife accused her of taking advantage of the community without contributing or sacrificing for the greater good, and Jessie pointed out to her brother that, as one of the Chroniclers, she possessed the same privilege as he did and could experience the outside world and return as she saw fit. She soon tired of the quarrels and secured the use of a small farm house in Iona, one of her old colleagues at the optometrist's inherited it from her parents and allowed Jessie to stay there whenever she needed, and it became her place of refuge.

Blake went back to the kitchen, began the coffee-making process again, thought about food and looked inside the fridge, in the squat pair of cabinets that housed his non-perishables, pulled out a bag of granola with no freshness remaining but not enough of a stale bite to keep him from pulling out handful after handful while the worn black mug slowly filled with steaming Viennese. A new assignment had come in while he'd been trawling the local sites, and he tried to work for an hour, researched insurer payment flexibility for Medicare and Medicaid procedures and started writing, but grew bored after 200 words. Someone in one of his movie threads had mentioned *Aaron Loves Angela*, and he hunted around until he found a bootleg online to download and watched the first 45 minutes, marveling at the drunken fury Ike invoked as he watched his old football highlights and lamented his fate and poured everything into Aaron.

None of the stories said murder, or homicide, or infanticide, or domestic abuse. None of them mentioned Tyner being arrested or charged with anything. All rumors, even the notion that he was a suspect came from an unnamed law enforcement source, and after some time Blake calmed down and went back to work. Finished all the research, outlined the rest of his article, and emailed the editor with his progress. The morning stretched into afternoon but from his vantage in the second floor apartment nothing much changed. Everything remained the same shade of mottled gray, the sky smeared with streaks of sad clouds, and he started to think about where, exactly, Tyner was holed up.

She looked like a model, like she didn't belong in Troy, didn't belong with Tyner, Jessie had always seemed, to Blake, like the incarnation of a small-town beauty, too good for everyone and everything around her. Sometimes he'd thought about her, when he drove back and forth to his warehouse job, when he walked home from the bar, when he sat alone in the apartment. He'd thought about her from the moment he saw her, thought about her white tank tops, her dark hair, thought about her seeing him the way other women did and finally saying yes to something much more real than what she'd given her life to.

He dressed for the weather, extra-thick socks, layered windbreaker pants, two shirts, a hoodie, and a sleek, waterproof jacket. For a moment, as he shivered in the driver's seat and tried to start the Camry, he worried the penetrating temperatures had affected his engine and he'd be stuck, but it turned over after the third twist of the key and he gave it a minute to warm up before taking off. He'd never understood Jessie's past or her reasons for betraying it all and becoming Tyner's possession, he wished she could see his dream for her, that living in a big city, moving away from Troy and from Tyner, would make her richer, happier, more beautiful, more everything.

The Hayes family was no longer in the Third Street apartment, they'd moved, after Jett arrived, into a one-story ranch within walking distance of the high school, and Blake crept through the snow-covered streets at 20 mph, the churning guitars and painful, otherworldly shrieks of Garry Shider inviting the devil to do the Cosmic Slop keeping him from drifting out of his lane, though thankfully the roads were mostly clear of other vehicles. The neighborhood looked familiar, not unlike the one he and Tyner had grown up in, though for Tyner it was merely one of many homes in his childhood, most of them wretchedly small or deprived of anything other than the basic necessities.

The house, set back just a little bit farther from the road than its neighbors, seemed to tumble out of sight, its back obscured by a sloping yard of hibernating grass. No cars in the drive, no lights, no warmth emanating from the inside, the only evidence of life was a pink plastic tricycle turned over on its side near the front door. Blake stopped the car in a little patch of clear asphalt out front and looked around. Maybe it was inevitable, he thought, that this family was doomed. Not in the manner it had occurred, he never expected such a brutal ending for Jessie and the kids. But Tyner had changed, was no longer interested in being a good friend, a good partner, or even a good person. He flaunted his side relationships, taking girls out to eat and to get drinks in Louisville and posing for pictures with them, texting on his regular phone with no regard for whether Jessie noticed what he was doing, staying overnight whenever and wherever he pleased.

After a few minutes he started to drive off, unsure what he expected, then stopped and opened his phone, went to Facebook and found the memorial page for Jessie and the kids. "I'll always remember Jessie, Jaz, Jett, and Georgy and this beautiful family, she loved them and made the world a better place by giving them to us, even for just a little while," he typed, then kept moving. The car skidded a little as he approached a stop sign, but he corrected and reminded himself to account for slower, longer, messier stops. He took turns without thinking, drove down streets he had no memory of, until he had crept out of the city and onto county roads that hadn't seen a plow or a touch of salt. The hills came into view, and the million dollar homes that dotted the tops of them, and he drove through a picturesque collection of hills covered in fine white powder that wouldn't have looked out of place in a European mountain range. Long, rangy curves pulled him deeper into the country, past expansive farms with endless wire fences and round hay bales slathered in snow and red two-story barns, past lone gas stations that encompassed the entire business and social activity of the little unincorporated communities he drove through.

A massive limestone tower rose above the treeline, gothic and beautiful and terrifying. A church. His chest began to vibrate, his heart thumping like he was actually inside the sanctuary, looking up at stained glass, looking at a fateful decision. He realized he was nearing St. Aureus, he was in Iona, though no sign told him anything until he came to the entrance of the campus. A long, winding drive led from the road and up to a set of beige buildings, their age indeterminate, but Blake recalled that St. Aureus was one of the oldest churches in southern Indiana still in operation, so he figured it had been built in the mid-1800s, not long after the first wave of Scottish and German immigrants began settling in the area. He drove into a small parking lot and stopped, gazed up at the imposing 150-foot tower, at the bejeweled cross welded to the very top, at the marble steps leading to the carved wooden doors at the entrance, and wondered how Jessie had ended up in such a holy, unsettling place.

Another road appeared, to the side of the main church, and he followed it, the sign indicating a hospitality center and gift shop and cemetery were ahead. The road swung past the buildings and into empty fields, nothing but fallow grass and soft little swells of land, until he saw the piece that had been designated the final resting place of first- and second-generation immigrants with names like Lubbehusen and Hauersbach and Schittersle. There's no creek out here, he thought to himself, and considered driving away, but another car came into view as he kept moving, a small Volkswagen parked along the side of the road, and winding through dozens of trees nearby was the yellow caution tape.

"She'll laugh when she reads the part that says I'm leaving," Isaac Hayes sang in his tough but sensitive baritone, and Blake pulled a dozen feet in front of the little black car and cut the engine, stepped out into the wintry mix of bone-clenching cold and piercing gusts and crunchy snow and peered into the wooded area. Long trails of tape affixed to maples and oaks and beeches flapped in the wind, and down a small ridge Blake could finally see the outline of the creek cutting through the landscape. He wasn't sure where the bodies had been found, the cordoned-off area covered most of the length of the creek in view and both banks and hundreds of square feet on either side and delved into the heavier woods where the ridge ended. And he suddenly felt uneasy about being there, if the sheriff's department had eyes on the area and was keeping tabs on people creeping around, he knew the stories of killers lurking near their crime scene to feel a sense of superiority, and he quickly got back into the car. A movement in the rearview mirror grabbed his attention and he turned around, the Volkswagen coughed to life and moved forward with its lights off, and as it passed him he glimpsed the driver. Long red hair, some of it tucked under a white snow cap emblazoned with a red W, blue eyes, a black leather jacket, and black leather gloves gripped the steering wheel. She didn't make eye contact with Blake, didn't seem to notice him or his car, her gaze looking right past him, into the woods.

Straight to Schwarz's, straight for the whiskey, and he looked around at the other bar-huggers, the sad-eyed, the paycheck-stompers, the exiled, and drained his glass, and asked for another, and kept asking until he couldn't any more.

Chapter 4

The pictures were so benign, so plain, and they nearly made Blake explode with nausea and anger. Snow everywhere, piled on top of Jazmin, on top of Jessie, in uneven clumps. The trees stark and menacing. The outline of footprints behind them. The baby, all alone.

A leak from someone, maybe a sheriff's deputy or someone in the coroner's office or the state police or even the FBI, there'd been gossip online that a local agent from Louisville had been called in to help with the investigation. It didn't matter, not to Blake, they'd been published, and he'd seen them, everyone could see them, the stiff little figures lying still and peaceful, Jessie's dark hair splayed out and peeking through the snow, her right arm stretched out, the bright, optimistic pink of Jazmin's jacket, and Georgy. Blake stared at the picture, zoomed in, the baby wasn't on his back, wasn't flopped over on his side, wasn't curled beneath his mother. He appeared to be sitting, his puffy legs out in front, arms to his sides, head up, almost tilted back, almost like he had fixed his gaze on something and never let it out of his sight.

Less than a week after the family's demise, and Blake still hadn't heard from Tyner or found a way to break the silence between them. The police were not actively seeking him, not publicly, but they wanted to know where he was and question him about things. Funeral arrangements were being made by Jessie's sister, who lived in Troy City but worked as a travel nurse and had to be called back from a job in Colorado and needed extra time to procure a replacement at the hospital and fly home. Blake wasn't sure about going to the funeral, hated the thought of seeing three little caskets arranged in a wood-paneled room at a funeral home. But I knew them, he thought, I have to go, I have to dive into the pain, no matter what.

It was time to eat. There wasn't a real closet in the apartment, the design had been haphazard and quick and no permit was secured, so after more than a year of draping clothes over the backs of chairs and stacking shirts and underwear and shorts in his upturned luggage, he'd bought a portable garment rack and slid it into a corner of the room. The plan had been to come back home, regroup, find a job, figure out his next move, and he hung his dress shirts and slacks and coats in preparation for interviews and meetings and cocktail hours. But nothing materialized, the clothes stayed put and grew more wrinkled, except for a couple of polo shirts and his fancier t-shirts that he didn't want to stuff into a bag. When his mom, Mariana, called for dinner, though, he skipped the sweats and logos and opted for clean clothes and whatever was available on the rack. The family dinners weren't held on a regular basis, not every Sunday or once a month, just whenever Landa and her mom felt like it.

After a moment of deliberation, Blake picked a long-sleeved blue shirt and jeans, walked across the snow and into his mom's house. He smelled the oil, the butter, the vinegar, and his mouth watered in anticipation. She was preparing his favorite meal, must have known he needed a little comfort, and he stepped into the kitchen and watched her for a few seconds, pounding pork cutlets, dredging them in egg and breading, checking the massive pot of red cabbage, and adding pepper to the bowl of mashed potatoes.

"Hi, Blake. You OK? Did you work today?" she said as he sidled up and took a long look at the food. He said yes, then moved to the little hutch in the dining room where the bottles of alcohol stood gleaming and beaming, just like where his dad kept them, just fewer in number and variety. The bourbon looked enticing and brown and sweet, more so than his mom's preferred cognac, and he poured several fingers into a heavy-bottomed glass just as Landa and Amos came into the house.

"Hey, Blake," Landa said somberly, and he nodded back, shook Amos' hand and went into the kitchen with them while Mariana finished cooking. After the death of her husband and the kids' father, she tried to make an effort to have them all eat in the dining room, to keep them connected and used to the little formalities that she believed made life as a family special.

"How's it going, you two?" Mariana asked as she added several pieces of pork to a heavy-bottomed skillet and stepped back to avoid the splatters of hot oil.

"OK. Busy with work, at least Amos has been." Landa began automatically pulling out dishes and glasses, Amos handled the silverware, and Blake stood awkwardly with his drink, then grabbed a fistful of napkins and took them to the dining room table.

"You guys want anything to drink? Mom, what do you have besides this liquor?" Blake called out.

"Nnnnnnothing for me, I have to be at wwwwwork real early," Amos said. After being around him more than five years Blake was used to hearing his brother-in-law stutter and occasionally get stuck on random words, but he remembered thinking, at first, that there was no way his sister could stand being with a guy who could barely hold up his end of a conversation. She promised Blake that in quieter moments his stutter practically disappeared, and it really only became pronounced when he was extremely stressed or nervous. Besides, she used to tell Blake, he's a good guy, he works hard all the time, he spends his free time at the gym and tackling projects at home, he volunteers with Big Brothers/ Big Sisters, he wants to have a big family, he was essentially the perfect man.

"Landa, wine? Mom, you got any wine?"

"I'm not drinking, Blake," Landa hollered back. He shrugged and poured some of the cognac for his mom, half the amount he'd given himself, and sat down in one of the heavily patterned chairs ringing the table while Mariana finished cooking and the table got covered in dishes.

They ate slowly and quietly, even though the schnitzel, mashed potatoes and red cabbage tasted as delicious as ever, but the cloud of death lingered over them until Blake broke the near-silence.

"So Amos," he started, paused and drained the rest of his whiskey, "are you working on the case up there? Is your department?"

"Well, I'm assssssisting the district commander and the Lieutenant Colonel in charge of crime scenes in southern Indiana, but it's a joint investigation with us and the sheriff's department. I'm basically helping with whatever they need, interviewing people and doing background and research."

"So it's definitely a crime scene, meaning they were murdered?"

"No, not nnnnnecessarily, but they want to make sure, not miss anything, it's too big a case to mess up."

"Who the hell did it, I mean, who does something like that to a bunch of kids? Are there any suspects?"

"I mean, I can't sssssssay anything about it." Amos took a long drink of water and looked at Landa. She knew something, she had to. "If it was a murder, then yeah, it's a person who obviously has no mmmmmorality. But it's just too soon to say anything right now."

"When's the last time you talked to Tyner?" Landa asked. Blake went back for more bourbon and sat down slowly, made sure not to look at his mom. She didn't say too much about what he did with his life, his missteps were well known and commented upon. She'd called his situation a disappointment when he came home from Ohio State, he anticipated her biting looks, cutting comments, frustrated sighs, and knew he deserved it all.

"Been a while, a text here or there back in the summer." Another slug of whiskey, a glance around the table, his eyes drawn to the dwindling collection of bottles in the hutch. "He's a busy guy, you know, we didn't really have time to get together, not like back in the day."

"Well, if you talk to him," Amos started, then swallowed something, a comment he knew he shouldn't say, and coughed into his fist, "let him know we're thinking of him, that we're sorry about what happened."

All he could do was finish his drink and slowly nod and start clearing the table, desperate to get out of there and get over to Schwarz's. Everyone brought in their dirty dishes and helped load the dishwasher and put things away, and Blake was ready to edge his way out the door and sprint through the snow and ice to get downtown.

"Hey, you guys leaving?" Blake asked Landa, who had gotten her purse and coat and was pulling on a pair of purple leather gloves.

"Um, yeah. Why?"

"Give me a ride downtown on your way home."

"Now? It's almost 10."

"I know, I'm supposed to meet someone there. A friend," he said quickly, in case she was set to ask him about a girlfriend or a date.

"OK, I guess. You ready?" She didn't wait for an answer, hugged and kissed Mariana and walked behind Amos to his silver Tundra.

Blake turned to his mom, smiled. "Well, thanks for dinner. My favorite."

"You're welcome. Don't stay out too late," she said, and he hopped down the slippery set of stairs and into the back of the cold truck.

"It's just down the way, on the corner of Everest and St. Joe's," he said to Amos. The music seemed off, at first, wailing, foot-stomping gospel that was clearly at odds with Landa's affinity for trap and southern-inflected beats and rhymes. Wait, he thought, they go to church now. A megachurch just on the outskirts of Troy City that had popped up in the few years since Blake left, came back, and fell into disrepair in the apartment. Her tastes and lifestyle had changed, clearly, and he hadn't bothered to notice or comment on any of it.

He thanked them for the ride and crunched along the sidewalk until he reached the front of Schwarz's. A thin crack ran up the middle of the front door, a reminder of the time Blake got shoved into the glass during a drunken argument. A simple, good-natured sports talk about basketball and overrated players, he'd thought, but the guy turned out to be a UK fan and didn't take kindly to Blake calling John Calipari a sports agent with a clipboard and claiming most of his players were busts, and he put two meaty hands into Blake's chest and pushed before the other guys in the place could pull him away. The brick walls were covered in random photos and cutouts and old gas station signs, the bar top seemed to shine unnaturally despite never getting much of a polish from whoever was pouring drinks, the orange tile floors never quite seemed clean enough, the tables were either too short or too tall, the booths felt cramped, the music leaned heavily in favor of classic and yacht rock, and the standard patrons, hard drinkers with soft bodies who favored bottled domestics and mid-shelf whiskey and classic two- and three-ingredient cocktails.

A spot at the end of the bar looked good, the TV was hanging nearby, there was a comfortable slab of brick to lean his back against when he turned his chair to the side, and he pulled up next to an empty seat that had a sweating beer in front. He pointed to the bartender, Casey, who nodded at him and got started on an old-fashioned made with Old Grand-Dad 114, no fruit. The intoxicating aroma hit Blake first, woodsy and sweet and chocolately and smokey, then the cool, biting alcohol, then the pleasant burn as it moved from the front of his mouth to the back and down his throat in a scintillating rivulet.

Just before the third sip, a hand clapped Blake heavy in between the shoulder blades, and he snapped his head around and saw the grinning face of Chris Blaine.

"What's up, white boy," Blake said, and made room for Chris to slide into his chair and turn to face him.

"Hey, mixey. What're you up to?"

"Drinking." They clinked glasses and turned their attention to the NBA game on TV and immediately began complaining about the quality of play and the stupidity of nearly everyone involved. For more than a year they'd been meeting at Schwarz's to drink and talk shit, though most of their meetings were happenstance and occurred less frequently as Blake and Clarke became more intertwined. But whenever Blake showed up, Chris was there, and vice versa.

"So you're here because your boy Tyner is out of pocket and his whole damn family is gone and you need to get fucked up." Chris chugged half his beer and slammed it on the thin coaster and nearly soaked it with lager residue. Casey looked up from the other end of the bar, he'd thrown Chris out of the place a couple of times, not for anything egregious or dangerous, just for being loud and stupid and getting on his nerves, but Blake wasn't in the mood for getting kicked out before he got obliterated on high-proof bourbon and bitters.

"Chill out with that, man," he said, and started to drink but held the glass a few inches from his lips, stared ahead. They could argue, raise their voices about trivial nonsense, and be OK, Blake knew that. They hadn't been friends in high school, they didn't hang with the same crowd, Chris occupied a rare strata, he was a blue-collar kid with a nice car and nice clothes who nonetheless found himself on the outskirts of the epic parties and never made inroads with Tyner or any of the popular athletes. Everyone knew him from elementary and middle school as a quiet, awkward kid with hand-me-downs and bad teeth, and never let him forget that just because his dad suddenly made a bunch of money and bought him a new Maxima when he turned 16 didn't mean he could infiltrate the cliques that had excluded him for so many years. But Blake always liked his attitude, he didn't care that he wasn't popular, didn't mind hanging with the kids with no money and no athletic achievements and no serious hope for ever getting out of Hudson County, he liked having a good time and drinking and smoking weed and listening to music in his Maxima at unholy levels. When Blake returned to Troy City and found the comfortable embrace of Schwarz's not too far from home, Chris was there, drinking beers and antagonizing old guys in stiff, dusty blue jeans who just wanted a drink after work.

"Alright, alright. But hey, I heard Tyner's been over in Louisville. You talked to him or seen him at all?"

"No, I haven't. Who said he's over there?"

"Come on, I got people, I know things."

"Whatever, if he was just up in Louisville the cops or somebody would have found out by now."

"Maybe." They both turned their attention to the TV for a few moments, observing the players do their thing, as much as they sometimes bashed them for this reason or that, they truly admired the craft, the physicality, and the unmatched talent of the guys, who made even a transcendent talent like Tyner appear to be a simple amateur the few times he attempted to play against them.

"So who's been talking about seeing Tyner? My brother-in-law is a cop and they don't know a damn thing about where he's at."

"I didn't say anybody's seen him, I said I heard where he was. People talk."

"What people?" Blake turned and looked hard at Chris, their repartee instantly put on hold, Blake not immune to copping an attitude with him.

"Just people, man, guys I know, they know some things and told me he's probably been hiding out with his boy."

"What boy? He's got a friend he's staying with in Louisville?"

"Nah, man, not a friend."

Chapter 5

He parked on Bonnycastle Avenue under a bare oak tree, the edges of Cherokee Park visible with some help from a flickering lamp down the street. No one had emerged from the terra-cotta shingled apartment complex in hours, only one window appeared illuminated from the street but he couldn't see much of anything inside, just the outline of a tall lamp and the golden frame of a modern-looking painting. A newer, nicer, taller building rose on the opposite side of the street, its penthouse condos offering, he assumed, dazzling views of the park and maybe even a decent look at downtown Louisville on a clear day.

No music, no audio book, no distractions. He always stayed focused, never failed in sticking to his task. The goal had been set a long time ago, the planning had begun a little more than two years earlier, although the new baby threw a small wrinkle into the mix, but he quickly adapted. The baby, the kids, wouldn't be a problem. "You must do it," he heard in his head. Again and again.

Movement in the window. He checked his phone, noted the time, almost 1 in the morning. A man's back, bare, a set of shoulders, long hair, thin gold necklace. He craned to see up into the apartment, rolled down the passenger's window to get a better look. A second back, a second set of shoulders. A second man.

Blake stared. Chris tried to ignore the heavy look, tried to drink his beer and stare at the TV, but gave up after just a few seconds.

"What?"

"You aren't gonna say anything else?" Blake asked.

"I'm telling you all I know. Guys I talk to, guys I do business with, they see shit, they hear shit, they tell me. That's it." Chris finished his beer and started to pull out his wallet, but Blake waved his hand in the air emphatically.

"Listen, man. You're perpetuating that old-school, down-low myth about black dudes, and that just doesn't happen the way people think it does," Blake said. "Wherever Tyner is, whatever happened to him, I don't think it's fair to start some nasty rumor and get people talking about him like he's somehow responsible for what happened to Jessie and the kids."

"I didn't say he was."

Blake stood up quickly, banged his chair into the brick wall, and tossed some money on the bar. He walked out without saying another word, didn't look at Chris or Casey or the group toasting each other with sloppy shots. The wind hit him as he pushed open the door, sometimes he forgot how devastating the winds could be this close to the river, how they rushed down the wide streets of downtown Troy and swirled around buildings and scattered random debris up into the air. The walk home took too long, the western wind driving into his chest and the ice causing little slips every few feet. By the time he made it into his apartment his lips had started to crack, his cheeks and nose were stiff, his mouth unable to move, and he didn't take off any clothes before moving into the kitchen, reaching around in one of the cabinets for a bottle, the only thing left an old, half-consumed Stoli from his dad's stash, and he poured some into a plastic cup, topped it with the rest of the coke he'd brought back from his shift at the warehouse a couple of days earlier.

The flat, varnish-like taste of his homemade cocktail caused an immediate clenching, his jaw, neck, eyes, innards, everything, but he did his best to quickly swallow all the brown dregs in the cup and get every drop inside of him. A dog barked, a throaty howl that rose up from the neighbor's yard right behind his apartment, a perky-eared, blue-eyed Malamute that had long ago become his least favorite animal on Earth and that he complained about frequently in random blog posts, though he'd never said a word to the owner. He made another drink, no mixer, just the vodka and some ice, plopped down on the couch and resumed his movie from a few days earlier. "So why do they call you Action?" Sharon Stone asked Carl Weathers just before a taxi drove straight at them and he yanked her out of the way and told her he had to catch a cab and initiated an insane chase sequence through the streets of Detroit.

The TV blurred with nonsensical action and one-liners and a couple more drinks that Blake consumed in quick succession. He picked up his phone, the screen blurry and packed with icons whose use had long since been forgotten. Scrolled through the messages. Found the name. Typed. "Ty. I'm sorry. I'll be at the service, talk to me, please."

He woke up a few hours later, a hot percolation keeping his head stuck to the pillow. Several minutes of effort were required to peel open his eyes, lift his body from the bed, trudge to the bathroom, and deposit the majority of last night's inhalations into the toilet. The service for Jessie and the kids was in the afternoon, and after a few minutes of cleaning himself up he realized he needed to get out the door, dressed and relatively sober, within 30 minutes if wanted to make it on time. Enough time for a quick shower, a hearty swirl of mouthwash, a swipe of a three-blade razor across his cheeks and down his neck, a search for something appropriate to wear to a funeral home. He couldn't find a plain, white dress shirt, so he chose a light blue one with sleeves that were just a bit too short, a navy jacket, and gray pants with just a whisper of wrinkle in the seam. Double-checked the location, Freeman's Funeral Home on Taylors Blvd., stepped out and failed, again, to account for the weather. The Camry roared to life and he slid the dial to defrost and cranked the temperature and fan as high as they would go, waited a minute, drove slowly through the familiar parts of Troy and into the East side. His playlist randomly pulled up some slinky funk by Twennynine, their biggest hit, and despite the circumstances and the frigid weather he found himself immersed in the call-and-response lyrics and sang, "If you're feeling hungry, ain't got nothin' to eat," near the top of his lungs as he drove past dilapidated car repair shops and warehouses and nail salons and BBQ spots and shuttered apartment buildings and businesses. He spotted a parking lot filled with cars and pulled over, then thought better of it and found a spot in the funeral home's lot. Deflated the music and the heat, checked the breast pocket and felt the outline of a long-hidden flask, pulled it out and took in just enough to ensure he wouldn't become a blubbering mess during the service.

The phone made a noise, a teasing bleep that he would normally have ignored, but something clicked in his head and he suddenly clawed through his pockets and found it, tapped a button and saw the message: "I'm here."

Chapter 6

No one moved. The heads had already swiveled, the gasps already exhaled, and Tyner and his mother stood reverently in the entrance to the chapel. He was resplendent in an all-black suit and freshly pressed white shirt, a small pair of glasses on his face, his fade and waves immaculate, his shoes glistening, as he held onto his mother's arm. She'd withered over the years, her frame no longer a reminder of where Tyner inherited his height, her hair no longer a magisterial crown of black curls and ringlets, just a dollop of white strands held together by a gold band. Despite Tyner's help she needed to use a walker and pushed it delicately down the aisle, the little tennis balls rubbing on the wood floor and creating an odd little squeak as they moved to the front row of seats.

Blake stood alone, didn't feel comfortable sitting with either Tyner's family or the few members of the Bochim community who'd come down for the service or the random people from throughout Troy City and Hudson County who felt compelled to show their faces, including city council members and the mayor and the chair of the hospital board and a columnist from the local paper and two reporters from Louisville TV stations. The little nuances of the service actually comforted him , the nearly inaudible gospel music piped into the room, the swiftly folded programs with Jessie and the kids' faces printed on the front, the perfect lines of chairs, the huge bouquets of flowers, the suits and dresses, the delicate quiet of every conversation. He almost smiled at Tyner's presence, at how it unnerved people and revealed something, their doubts, their fears, even their hatred. They suspected Tyner, at least some of them did, he could tell by their reactions, their expressions, the curl of their mouths into little sneers, the tightening of their eyes, the cupped hands around their lips as they whispered to a neighbor. What they suspected, Blake wasn't sure, because there didn't appear to be any scrap of evidence in the investigation that hinted anyone was involved.

A pastor read some verses from the Bible, offered healing in his way, and a friend of the family sang an acapella version of "Jesus Promised Me a Place Over There" and nearly fell over out of breath as he wailed, "No more sickness, sorrow, pain, because He promised me a home over there." A few more words, banal comfort to those who had to recognize the pain the children must have gone through in their final moments, and then the line of grievers began their march past Jessie's sister and Tyner and his mother. Blake waited, he let almost everyone go first to offer their condolences, he wanted extra time, needed that moment with his friend. But when he shuffled through, when he stood in front of him, all he could do was reach in for a hug, a real hug, and hold on for as long as he possibly could.

He trailed the assemblage of mourners out to the lobby, and his discomfort was almost vulgar in its immediacy, forcing him to nod his way outside instead of saying a word to anyone. A thin dusting of snow covered his windshield and roof, and he got into the car and turned on the wipers, and as the view cleared he saw a woman a few vehicles over, red hair, blue eyes, leather gloves, getting into the same little Volkswagen he'd seen near the crime scene in Iona. Her hair swooped down a long white coat, all the way to the middle of her back, the red so bright against the coat. If you see enough women, Blake thought, then you notice all the little details, all the things that make them unique and special. He watched her drive away, away from Troy City and towards the highway that led to Louisville, and he shed his coat and shifted to D to follow, but Tyner walked out with his mom and Jessie's sister and a handful of others, and a gray hearse backed up to a door and he saw the four caskets loaded inside by a few of the Freeman workers.

Purple flags were stuck to the roofs of about a dozen cars, and they crept behind the hearse with their hazard lights on and slowly worked their way out of the parking lot. Blake followed at a distance, not willing to let himself be a part of the service, and after 10 minutes the line of cars pulled through the gates of Hudson County Memorial Gardens. A rock archway curved over the entrance, and a pair of stone angels stood on either side, one holding its hands in supplication, the other resting its head on a rectangular slab. He drove past and pulled onto a sliver of gravel next to the road, not sure what he was doing, not sure why he didn't just go home. There were no assignments in his inbox to work on, no shifts he'd scheduled, no recent messages from Clarke, he wasn't on the verge of anything in his life or his world, the only thing that orchestrated movement within him was the confusion and rage surrounding Tyner's family.

A car drove by, slowly, a small gray Toyota truck, its back bumper slightly askew, and Blake watched it for longer than he realized. It came to a stop a few hundred feet past his Camry, the brake lights blazing bright and red through the fluttering snowflakes. Stayed parked there, almost menacing in its brazen stillness. Something's up with that truck, Blake thought, and when it started its slow ascent, Blake trailed behind, not too close, not too far, the tracks in the snow giving its position away too easily. They moved away from the cemetery, away from Troy City, toward Bochim, the route not familiar but its remoteness a telltale sign.

The hills rose and fell, the ravines gouged the earth, the homes grew smaller and more functional, and Blake began to wonder about the people who'd occupied those parts of Hudson County for generations. The farmers and their families, the hard-working white people of Europe and the eastern United States who'd left whatever desperate situation they'd been in to stake their claim and their lives on unknown plots of land in a relatively unknown state. They weren't bad people, they couldn't be, they'd toiled and scrounged and scrapped and made a living out there, but he'd also experienced too much bullshit from the kids who'd grown up away from Troy, the country boys and girls who lived on farms and drove extra-long flatbeds and were too quick to denigrate him for being different. He could forgive, to a certain point, but not forget.

The road started to thin, it seemed impossible for multiple cars to pass at the same time, and the trees thickened and felt like they were growing up and over the small line of asphalt they were driving on. He realized he hadn't seen a sign in miles, nothing to indicate which direction he was headed, what the road was named, where exactly he was. "You may not have, a car at all," the sugary baritone crooned from the speakers as he rounded a curve and seemed to lose sight of the truck. There were no turn offs, no driveways or roads that he could see, just an endless demarcation of pines and spruces and cedars stretching into the muffled gray sky. The road continued its gentle arc around a small knob, and Blake slowed, tried to get a read on the land, where things started and stopped, how anyone could live in a place that seemed so desolate.

He couldn't have explained where he was if someone had asked, and assumed if he kept driving he'd wind up in some other county, probably LaGrange, to the north, and pulled over to the side of the road and turned off the engine. Cut off the music. Pushed his face into the wheel, his forehead growing numb by the second as the seams pressed into his skin, his mouth slightly ajar, sour breath blowing into the instrument panel and clouding the glass. His exuberance had faded into nothing, his unexplained task evaporated, and he breathed harder, his eyes began to water, and he wiped the tops of his cheeks with the edge of his too-short shirt sleeve. None of his troubles seemed to matter, nothing he'd done up that point in his life, all 27 years, meant a thing anymore.

A wave of pressure suddenly rolled through his abdomen, he realized he hadn't taken a piss since waking up, and he pushed open the door and walked around to the passenger's side, continued through the crunchy patch of grass to the line of trees, stopped, then took a few steps into the woods. Unzipped, pulled himself through the layers of fabric, sprayed the base of an unsuspecting maple while he looked up and around. Something caught his eye, a metallic twinkle, unnatural amidst the sea of bark and branches and trunks surrounding him, and he finished up and squinted into the direction of the glimmer he'd seen.

Nothing at first. Then it sparkled, again, and he moved out of the trees and tried to look closer, but it was too far away to see much of anything. He jogged back to the car, started it up and spun it around to head back where he'd come from, about 500 yards or so, and pulled off to the side facing the nonexistent oncoming traffic. Got out and stared at the trees, saw what had been catching the light, a small bundle of geodes dangling from a fishing line, their crystal interiors throwing off sparkles from the rays of sun that managed to creep through the gloomy afternoon sky.

A chill slipped into his Kenneth Cole's as he bustled through the grass again and got closer to the rocks hanging from the limbs of a gigantic oak that seemed to stretch hundreds of feet into the air. Large branches spiraled in every direction, and as he got closer he saw little figures in the bark. Symbols. His fingers touched the largest, a circle with a dot in the middle. An eye.

A shadow crossed over the top of Blake, hovered and quivered in a dark mass against the tree. He looked up, the sky was empty, just the color of ennui floating by, then started to turn, a simmering, low rush of breath suddenly audible. Someone was standing right behind him, and he started to speak, to explain, but stopped. The man, the person, the thing, towered over Blake, nearly 7-feet of sinewy arms and legs covered by denim overalls and a long white shirt. A pair of tiny, pulsing blue eyes stared out of an oversized, square head topped by a blonde crew cut, and his mouth hung open, the teeth inside feral and caked in plaque, the tongue nearly white and pushing against his lower lip.

Blake opened his mouth to say something, to apologize or explain what he was doing, but the giant raised a claw-like hand and pointed a bony finger in his face. "You," he said, and Blake recoiled, the voice so wispy and high-pitched that it seemed phony coming out of such an ogreish face. "Leave. Or I'll kill you."

Chapter 7

The finger was inches from Blake's nose, and he stared at it but didn't move, despite the threat. Is this guy, this thing, really real, he thought, and after a few more seconds backed against the tree and raised his hands.

"Sorry, I just got lost and had to use the bathroom. I'm going." He scooted around the trunks of the trees with his arms still up and his eyes fixated on the miniature blue irises piercing him with a predatory hatred he had never encountered. Backed through the grass, still looking, and wondered how a person of such monstrous size and irregular shape could have snuck up on him through dead brush and crackling ice and snow. He got into the driver's seat, not quite shaking but definitely a little rattled by the confrontation, and started the car, spotted the guy still standing by the trees, staring, and pulled onto the road, careful not to peel out and appear too afraid. After a few seconds he looked in the mirror to see where the enormous thing was. Gone.

By the time he parked on his street, walked up the steps and into his apartment, tore himself out of his formal attire and sat down in heavy blue sweatpants and an oversized black Mizzou hoodie, his adrenaline and nerves had receded into normal territory, but he still needed something. Fumbled around on the coffee table until he found his pen and inhaled as much as he possibly could, then slumped back on the bed with the TV stuck on one of the sports channels that played nothing but old college football and basketball games.

For several minutes in his slightly fuzzy state he considered what to do for the remainder of his day, then took 15 minutes to write an elegy to Jessie and the kids that he posted to his blog. His life felt like it was too difficult to escape, the moments too random and useless to mean anything, but he could only watch himself giving in, couldn't do much of anything except trudge through the hours with a smile and a promise to himself that maybe he'd find a way to rise above the mediocrity and the nothingness to find a place for his talents and his mind.

He thought about Troy City, the place he'd come back to not long after Tyner did. It always felt so small to him, and it wasn't a big place, wouldn't register with anyone who didn't know about the school's basketball exploits or its relative proximity to the more pleasurable and impactful Louisville. For so long he knew he was too good for his hometown, he'd get out and go to college and then medical school and then go practice in a thriving metropolis like Chicago or Nashville or Indianapolis, someplace he could escape to and yet still be somebody special. Then the night happened, and he knew the only place that would take him, the only place he could go, was home. They'd forgive him, his mom, his sister, his friends, everyone. He could restart, rebuild, whatever it took and however long it took, Troy was the place to do it. Along with forgiveness, though, came a lack of pressure, and he knew he had allowed himself to succumb to the ease of his life, sleeping too long, writing for tidy little sums of cash, pushing a cart around a warehouse, accepting dalliances with Clarke only when she felt like it, ignoring the tension in his chest and the holes in his soul.

The light dimmed outside, and he grabbed for the remote and turned to a channel with live sports. Basketball. Players that were better than Tyner in every way, but who lacked his spirited approach to the game, his wild forays to the basket, his creative passes, his big smile that flashed any time he felt good, which was just about every minute he was on the court. He was a star, a legend, Blake thought, because of how he made people feel when they watched him.

They didn't care about that in Bochim, though. The mysterious little community, which sprung up in the late 1960s as a place of free will and sharing and idealism about the natural world and how people should live with one another, was founded by a group of ex-college students from California who'd migrated east and never left. For a few years the members lived relatively peacefully amongst themselves in the place they initially called Potters Hill, with big shared meals at an extra-long outdoor table nearly every day, and large projects, like digging drainage ditches and building small structures and cutting roads through the woods, were treated as an endeavor for all to work on. Many people lived in canvas-covered lodges and heated them by fire, others built small homes into the sandstone hillsides, nearly everyone contributed to the vegetable and fruit gardens, and a couple of older men managed plots of farmland and grew soybeans, corn, and wheat. There were too many druggies, though, single guys who were more interested in smoking weed and dropping acid than participating in any sort of hard labor that would benefit their neighbors, and after five years the community seemed destined to collapse.

Some say he had been there all along, others say he emerged as Potters Hill began its rapid descent, but by the middle of the 70s, as the ex-students drifted off to the normal world and the remaining members were trying to determine whether or not to continue, the man who came to be known as Bezalel became a leading voice in the community. He began to speak about the evils of drug use, the wasted potential of those who failed to function as workers or contributors, and soon all drugs and alcohol were prohibited. When Bezalel predicted that an imminent storm would wash away the upcoming wheat crop and foresaw the birth of two sets of twins, the members began to believe in his visions, his teachings, and his principles. He renamed the town Bochim, filed paperwork with Hudson County to avoid the citizens having to pay taxes, wrote a constitution, elected six men as senior council members, with him as the leader, and imposed strict regulations on anyone who wished to live in the community. From his personal funds he spent thousands of dollars on carpentry and lumber equipment and appointed his friend, Daniel McQueen, as the overseer of a lumber mill that generated over $100,000 a year in pooled income that soon allowed the town to become self-sufficient.

The laid-back, secular, hippie quality of the original Potters Hill gave way to a rigorous life of work and worship, all overseen by Bezalel, Daniel, and Bezalel's wife, May, who was in charge of the midwives and the mothers and the children and the production of all the community's food. For the first few years of Bezalel's leadership the community met on Sunday mornings and evenings for his talks and predictions in a small, simple picnic area originally built by the college students. But he had the spot razed, ordered the men to dig a ½ acre pond on the site, and utilized the lumber mill profits to purchase two semi-truckloads of limestone blocks from Oolitic for the construction of a stone sanctuary deep in the woods. He baptized members on the shores of the pond and conducted all services in the two-story sanctuary, where the emphasis for all centered on purity of the body and the soul. May gave birth to three children in a span of five years, the two boys, Issachar and Manasseh, and Bilhah, who later changed her name to Jessie.

Tyner never said much about the place to Blake. He'd been there once to pick up Jessie and the kids at a small brick house where they'd been staying for a week while he traveled for work. A tiny, gray-haired woman on a four-wheeler escorted him to the house after he reached the front entrance, which was just a pair of black utility gates secured with a chain, nothing more elaborate than you'd find on any farm in Hudson County. The road, mostly dirt with a hint of gravel peeking out, wound its way past small clusters of people working odd jobs, kids playing with dogs and frisbees, trucks and tractors driving slowly but purposefully through a labyrinth of roads winding through the trees. The stories he'd heard, that he and Blake and countless others in Troy had grown up with, didn't seem to be anything to take seriously, all he could see of the place indicated it was a simple community of farmers and laborers and kids. When the woman pulled her four-wheeler to a stop, Tyner pulled behind her in his SUV and watched Jessie emerge from the house with the kids and the bags, swept up the little ones in his arms and kissed Jessie, but felt a swarm of eyes on him from every direction, even though the only other person in sight was the escort. They drove off alone, and Tyner never saw the place again.

Blake didn't know what to think of his own encounter. The isolated road. The stark, bleak woods. The rocks strung up in the trees. The imposing, angular, stealthy, blonde giant who'd threatened him. As his head started to clear, he pulled his computer onto his lap and opened all the social media accounts he could find for both Tyner and Jessie. Most posts from Tyner were about playing ball, hobnobbing with people around town, shaking hands with fans, pictures of the kids, pictures of him from his high school and college glory days. Nothing much about Jessie.

He started digging, found Jessie's pictures and posts from a couple of defunct sites from several years earlier, she seemed to maintain a basic online presence elsewhere, highlighted mostly with posts about her life as a mom and part-time worker and Tyner's partner. No mention of Bochim or her father or anyone else from the community. A glut of pictures and comments from Jazmin's baby days, "Mommy's eyes and daddy's lips, so cute," "Such a pretty girl!" "Proud momma!" "I will love her every day forever!!!!" Not as much about Jett, mostly pictures of her with her big sister and Tyner, the arrival of a little boy seemed to spark something in Tyner and he popped up, smiling, in nearly every image of the kid.

Things started to change in the months leading up to her death. The tone. The intensity of her emotions. Friends left comments on many of the posts, but they seemed more interested in cheering her efforts as a mom than getting into the psychology of what she was saying. "I really don't know what I'm waiting for," she wrote in the first post that made Blake pause. Then he kept reading.

"I'm too messed up."

"All that for nothing."

"No waiting, get it over with."

"I don't know why I'm like this."

"We never have the answers why things just happen."

"No waiting, no hesitating, no excuses."

"They will never be alone."

"I am in the worst place, and it's getting to me everyday."

"I am determined. Today."
"Done with thinking."
"I know what I have to do."

Chapter 8

Great piles of snow lay in the yard between Blake's apartment and the house, the kind he would have delighted jumping in as a kid while his mom laughed from the kitchen window and prepared mugs of hot chocolate for him and Landa. He'd make snowmen if he didn't succumb to the cold and go inside too quickly, always so anxious to show them off to his dad, who had grown up down south and professed not to have seen a snowflake until he was almost 30 years old. But Blake never got to show him a completed, fully erect snowman in the yard, they had melted or been deformed by the time he made it home to the family.

There were a lot of gaps in Blake's knowledge of his parents' history together. His dad, Nelson Prince, joined the Army after two years of community college in Georgia, and utilized the G.I. Bill and earned a Doctor of Osteopathic Medicine degree and became a family medicine practitioner. Part of his Army travels took him to Fort Knox, which made him familiar with Louisville, and made him familiar with physicians in the area. He eventually opened a full-time practice, Prince Pediatrics, in Troy City, while also maintaining privileges at a couple of hospitals in Louisville. Nelson was, in fact, the first African-American doctor to practice in Hudson County, and though he experienced some pushback from a handful of pediatricians in the city who did not want him taking any of their business, he thrived with a small office close to the east side of Troy for more than 20 years.

Blake's mom, Mariana, grew up in Germany but moved to the United States as a teenager to live with an aunt and go to college in Virginia. She met Nelson, who was almost 10 years older than her, when he was nearing the end of his first year of residency at a clinic outside Chesapeake . They got married quickly, and Blake and Landa were both born as Nelson was building his practice in Troy.

Other than those basic biographical details, Blake knew very little, and always felt uneasy about delving too deeply into their relationship. He didn't know where, exactly, they met, or what prompted them to jump into marriage so soon, or why Mariana moved to the U.S. at age 17 when her father was a well-to-do chemist and businessman. He'd always waited for some kind of explanation from either of them, but that never materialized, and he only had his observations of the two of them together. Their stilted but respectful banter. Their light touches of affection. Their looks across the dining room table over a glass of wine or whiskey.

During Blake's freshman year of college at Rose-Hulman, a private school in Terre Haute, Nelson died. No reason was initially given by Mariana when she called Blake, just that his dad was sick and he needed to come home as soon as possible. A stroke, someone told him when he finally made it back to Troy, a word and malady he'd heard so many times but actually knew nothing about despite growing up in a house with a doctor. Nothing could be done by the time Blake made it home, his dad lingered for a day after checking into the hospital and then he disappeared, the breath and the life wafted out of Nelson's body and all that remained was a husk that Blake could barely recognize as his father.

He looked out the small window of his apartment at the snow, heard the Malamute whining and whimpering next door, and returned his attention to the computer. A new playlist had begun and he tapped the volume key on the laptop, nodded his head to the funky rhythm and high-pitched vocals of Narada Michael Walden belting out, "I should have loved ya." He wanted something, a touch of organization to the rampant speculation and nonsense he found online. One blogger swore that Tyner had been seen in Iona by a farmer the morning of the deaths, a thread on Twitter perpetuated a rumor that Jessie was addicted to prescription pills and was going out in the morning to meet a dealer, got high and wandered in the snow with her kids. The crime reporter for the Troy City *Herald-Bulletin* posted a handful of updates to her feed about the ongoing investigation but offered nothing of substance or note. Mariana texted him to ask if Tyner was really the father of the kids. Lies, as far as Blake could tell, but he knew he couldn't dismiss any of it. As much as he'd valued his friendship with the boys through the years, the things they'd shared, the trust they'd shown in one another with secrets and vulnerabilities, all that remained was a collection of words and memories, and Tyner, Blake realized, was likely capable of anything.

But something has to be coming, he thought as he sat with the computer propped on a pillow next to him. It was too soon for autopsy or toxicology results, and there was no way the police were going to release anything to the public. He let his eyes and his mind wander. To his two biology courses in med school, to chemistry, to stories he'd gathered in his limited research and conversations with his dad. Words and terms poured in; core temperature, adrenergic, thermal homeostasis, rewarming, coagulation. He tried to pin them down, give them context or a chance to lead to a path he could follow, but they spun away, leaving him with nothing.

He did his best not to think about his time in Columbus. Medical school. The dream. The hope. The fulfillment of so many wishes, so much blood and life spilled by the generations that came before him. Nelson was the start, and Blake was supposed to be the continuation, the next piece, but it never happened. Never would. He'd given it a shot, changed from a laid-back student to a serious scholar, and eschewed the nonchalance that bloomed all around him the last two years of high school, smashed the thresholds for scores and grades and measurables, sailed through undergrad with a near-perfect resume, and prepared himself for seven or eight years of exhaustion and academic and physical torment. And he did it all with an eye toward a future of dignity and privilege and wealth.

It didn't take too long for him to realize that, despite his departure from Ohio State, the time he'd spent there and his undergrad credentials and his connections with more successful friends could lead to the kind of work that would enable him to earn some money, give his days some meaning and some purpose, and keep his mom off his back. He emailed and harangued enough people to get a chance to freelance for a few online magazines, work that was easy enough but let him continue to be a part of the world. In some way.

He looked around, spotted the books. From time to time he glanced around his apartment absentmindedly, after a few drinks or a few puffs, and came across the handful of medical texts that remained in his possession. None from his time at OSU, he'd sold those almost immediately for a little bit of cash. They were his dad's. *Wilderness and Environmental Medicine.* Various *Merck* manuals. An out-of-print *DSM*. A fairly new copy of *Harrison's Principles of Internal Medicine.* Something always came over him when he let his gaze rest on those books. Guilt. Anger. Jealousy. Acceptance. He'd never use them, not like they were meant to, but he'd always keep them, he realized one day. Worthwhile or not, they were a part of who he was. Or what he would have been. His dad was important, Blake knew that and always would, the remnants of his father's life far more validating than anything he could do. But he wanted to try.

A ping from somewhere, the phone, at 10:30 only one person would attempt to reach him, and after attempting to stand up he was positive he'd be unable to effectively operate a motor vehicle or a zipper or anything with moving parts. He plopped back down and tried to think of a lie, scanned his shelves until he found something worth watching in his current state, and laughed like an idiot at the fuzzy VHS copy of *Let's Do It Again* that his dad made him sit through as a kid.

The dim light of the TV slowly woke him, he uncrooked his neck from its odd position and strained his eyes to find the time on a nearby device. He'd fallen asleep before the rematch between Bootney Farnsworth and 40th St. Black, but of course knew the outcome and knew Sidney and Bill ended up raising the money for their fraternal order. A slim line of moonlight illuminated part of the floor, and he followed it to the bathroom and took care of business in the dark, followed with a swish of mouthwash and a quick scrape of his battery-powered brush against his teeth. Another light, the phone, the nagging little dot letting him know he'd missed a call or message and it wouldn't go away until he handled it.

"Don't say a thing to anyone." Blake squinted at the phone, unsure who'd sent the text, the number unfamiliar and his eyes still adjusting. "Look close then delete," the second message read.

Another message. Pictures. Snow-covered earth. Trees. A bubbling creek. The bodies.

Chapter 9

The fury increased inside of him. Doubled, tripled, grew so large and so fierce until it threatened to block out any of the light remaining inside of him. He sat alone, the only company his mind seeking answers from God about how worthy he'd been, how much more was required until he could put an end to the tenacity tearing through his soul. And it all started again.

Clarke would be angry, Blake knew, he'd bowed to her too many times, in too many ways, for a missed opportunity like the previous night to do anything other than force her to act out in her own simple and dangerous manner.

But he was unable to think about Clarke's scorn. Not after seeing the photos. The faces of the children, serene and frozen. Jessie's visage, still irresistible in its paleness and softness. All of their hair strewn and messy. All of their eyes closed.

For a few minutes he shut everything down, slammed the lid of the laptop, buried his face in a pillow, disgusted with himself for daring to look, once again, into the last lonely act of their little lives. But he'd fallen into a spell, a macabre trance of peering into the face of death in a way he never had before. He never saw his father's body after he passed, there was no backroom visit in the hospital, in the funeral home, no open casket. Even his time in medical school failed to provide the up close look at a cadaver, as he'd left before the start of gross anatomy and the grim rite of passage of cutting into a body for the purposes of edification.

The pictures of the surroundings revealed nothing but sky, hibernating branches and limbs, vast white emptiness beyond the pockets of forest and woods that clung near the creek winding through Iona and the St. Aureas campus. He began to recognize things from his recent drive up there, a clump of bushes, the curve of the creek as it pushed its way past a rocky embankment, fallen trees with a ridge of flaky snow on top. The place conjured nothing, on its own, but as Blake looked at the pictures he sensed something, a majesty and power and aura that confirmed it had seen life, and taken it.

Then there were the kids. He hadn't known them, their faces or their moods or their personalities, though he'd been around Jazmin the most those first months of her life while he and Tyner were still relatively close. She seemed darker, he even remembered Jessie commenting on how light the little girl's skin had once been, but blackness always finds a way, Landa's skin in her baby pictures looked nothing like it did as an adult. Blake seemed to be the exception, he'd been mistaken all his life for any number of ethnicities, nationalities, races, Brazilian, Hispanic, Spanish, Italian, Hawaiian, Mexican, Greek, Egyptian, white. The little ones were lighter than Jazmin, barely resembled Tyner, until he saw their noses, the wide nostrils and short bridges, and the tight curls that could only have come from their black father.

Jessie. She seemed to glow in the photo, not just because of her white skin, but the way her soul seemed alive, at last, instead of hidden behind makeup and false cheer and the scrutiny's that ate at her constantly. Being with Tyner. Having his kids. Being a mom. Being from Bochim. She looked safe from suffering and the impositions of her life. She looked free.

Blake had no idea where the photos had come from, who'd messaged them surreptitiously in the middle of the night with a plea to keep quiet and destroy them as soon as possible. He tried a reverse-lookup of the number, found nothing, tried to parse the few words in the message and determine who could have written them, but had no answer. The grimness had worn off of the pictures and he glanced at all of them a few more times, familiarizing himself with the details, the depth of the gray in the sky, the clothes, the glitter of gold in Jessie's ears and on her neck. Then noticed the lack of headwear on any of them, the lack of gloves, the lack of winter boots. He peered closer and saw feet. No one, not Jessie, not the kids, was wearing shoes.

He tapped the first picture, found the delete icon, sent it into the nether regions of his phone, and did the same for the rest, he could have kept them or saved them somewhere else but decided to listen to whomever had sent them. But before he could eliminate the final one, the picture of Jessie, he paused, used his fingers to zoom in. The necklace, a simple gold chain with small links, he'd been with Tyner at the Jefferson Mall in Louisville, saw him pay $74.39 in cash for it, and Tyner gave it to Jessie on her 20th birthday not long before she left her family and community. The necklace measured 20 inches, not that long, and rested just above the light blue shirt she'd worn under her winter coat. And attached to the chain, barely visible, unmistakable, was a small gold cross.

Chapter 10

First he paced. Around and around in oddly spaced circles across the main room of his apartment. Who do I call, who do I tell this to, he thought after a few dozen laps. It mattered, what he'd seen, and he wondered if anyone would understand when they saw the cross, know of its unnatural presence on the end of that necklace, or if everyone would assume it belonged there, had always been there, and would sweep it for fingerprints and then toss it in a plastic bag.

Amos. He'd need to know the importance of the necklace and the cross, could relay the information to his superiors, who'd alert all the higher-ups and set in motion the kind of detailed, determined investigation the case needed. Experts and scientific equipment called in. Manpower, dozens of cops sweeping the hillside and interviewing friends and neighbors and planting informants and collecting the most minute pieces of evidence. The incident would draw more than just the prurient side of the news, it would spark an even bigger outcry and create a more sensitive look into what happened to the family.

Then he stopped moving, placed a hand against the thin drywall and bent his head. No, he couldn't tell anybody. If there were thoughts that what had occurred with the family was not merely a tragic accident but some kind of premeditated attack, suspicion would instantly land on Tyner, even more than it already had. And the fact that it would come from Blake, his friend, would lend it even more seriousness and credibility. All at once, he realized the discovery, the epiphany, was nothing more than a test, a curse that would damn him and his friend if he ever said a word.

Not enough sleep, not to function like a working adult, but he had no choice. He shelved the idea of telling someone about the cross, turned on his laptop, saw the new assignment, made coffee, ate a bowl of cereal, and plowed into researching health care initiatives being debated in several state houses around the country. He hated writing those stories, always detested the language of elected dummies pretending to understand anything about medicine or treatment or the human body. But he had no room to complain, the money continued to be pretty steady, and for one of the few moments of his day he could flex some of the knowledge he'd gleaned from his time at OSU. That was something he hated and regretted. Not a doctor. Not respected. Not admired. Not rich. Not brimming with intelligence and smarts and skills.

Four hours passed at the computer, his brain simmering and functioning at a pretty high rate for the first time in weeks, maybe months. He paused to eat, realized he didn't have much in the way of fresh food, put on shoes and a black-and-red Buckeyes windbreaker and slipped into his mom's kitchen for whole wheat bread and raspberry jam and the only unbruised Gala apple in the basket Mariana kept on the counter. No matter how little he shopped, he made sure to keep peanut butter in his little one-cabinet pantry so he could at least slather whatever bread he had with some non-stir crunchy and make a quick sandwich. Crumbs fell on the table, on the floor under him, on his t-shirt emblazoned with the logo for Riehr End Drugstore, a silly place he saw on a drive home when he was an undergrad.

Not long after Shaft survived the assassination attempt from Mascola, in the sequel that no one ever talked about but Blake found superior to the original, if for no other reason than the presence of Moses Gunn, he returned to the computer, spent 10 minutes browsing news sites, he'd skipped doing it earlier and felt somewhat off after missing out on one of his new morning rituals. He didn't want to, but he clicked on an article on one of the news channels' sites, even though he knew there was probably no new info being doled out to the media and there was no reason for an updated story. But he took the time to leave a comment, writing "There's more to this story than anyone is willing to say out loud, hopefully the police start looking at what's really going on," and he did it all with his name and photo from Facebook.

At the top of the page, his eyes landed on another article, the headline reading simply, "Police investigating young woman's death." An innocuous enough title, considering the heaviness of the subject matter, and he tapped on the link, read about a 21-year old from Fern Creek named Chantelle Billings discovered behind a half-abandoned strip mall on Poplar Level Rd. Not much in the way of details, only the time her body was found, the nearest intersection, the fact that no cause of death had been determined, an autopsy was pending, there were no suspects, no witnesses. A similar title on the page appeared, a similar story, a young woman, Venture Mitchell, 22, found behind a pizza place on Berry Blvd. Another story, another woman, Tiarrah Boyd, 27, gas station on Algonquin. He knew it instantly from the names, the locations, they were all young black women, but it took him longer, with more research and more reading and more coffee, to find himself realizing something more concrete. All three had, at some point, been dancers in some of the less reputable strip clubs along 7th. Street Rd. They'd all been arrested for or suspected of prostitution or soliciting. They each had small children.

Four dead women, including Jessie, in three months. Perhaps all the women were destined to suffer, to endure, to create life, to love their children, to lose them in some way. Blake couldn't find much more information about the dead women in Louisville, no follow-up stories about expanded investigations, increased police patrols in the areas where the women were found, calls to state and federal task force members for additional assistance. They lived on the fringes, they died on the fringes, and no one really seemed to care. Maybe they'd forged lifelong friendships, maybe they lived in fear of an enemy they'd made, maybe they went to church regularly, an AME or Baptist sanctuary favored by their grandmother, maybe they drifted away from God at some point and never recovered, maybe they made everyone around them laugh, maybe they caused nothing but pain. It didn't matter, they were dead black girls from Louisville, from the wrong neighborhoods. They were there, and then they were gone.

There were some African Americans who lived in Troy City, not very many, maybe 9 or 10 percent of the total population, they didn't sway elections or infiltrate seats of government, but their presence extended further than the basketball courts. Blake wasn't sure what brought the first black folks across the river to Hudson County, he didn't know anything about migration patterns, he was not a descendant of those people, but Troy certainly looked and behaved differently than so many other little Indiana towns up and down the Ohio River. Tyner was one of those descendants, his family was, and so many others had lived and worked there for decades, but Blake, in a lot of ways, was still an outsider. He wasn't the exact same color, didn't grow up in the same kind of house, under the same circumstances, with the same restrictions and history. The plight of those women in Louisville felt as personal as an earthquake in Guangzhou or a monsoon in Mumbai.

Only one of the stories showed a photo of the victim, but a quick search turned up a few images, and when he saw a shot of Tiarrah Boyd from the side, with her arms bare and visible in the bright sun, he leaned in closer. A large cross was tattooed across her deltoid and biceps. He hunted for photos of Chantelle and Venture, there were plenty, pictures with their children, at parties, in front of a house, on the sidewalk, at a club. No necklaces or crosses of any kind, he kept looking but came up empty. He texted Amos quickly, who could likely guess what Blake was up to but couldn't definitively say anything to his bosses about what was happening. "Hey, u able to access pics from crimes in Lville?" An urgency must have crept into his words that Amos detected, who wrote back in less than two minutes, "I can, names/s?" After getting the spelling correct, Blake sent the names, first and last, to Amos, found his vape pen and noticed there wasn't much left in the cartridge, decided it was best to eliminate the remaining, and proceeded to inhale and exhale for nearly 10 minutes before he finished it all. He put his head on the pillow and flipped on a movie, and giggled incessantly at the antics of the employees of the Dee Luxe Car Wash, although he turned the movie off, as always, when Abdullah and Lonnie engaged in their big dramatic scene at the end.

In the early morning hours he awoke with his face nearly velcroed to the pillow, peeled himself away and drained his bladder with the lights off. He needed more sleep, real sleep, grabbed the phone to set an alarm for 10 o'clock, but saw a text from Amos, rubbed the gunk from his eyes and opened up the message. The photos weren't gruesome like he expected, there was no blood or gore or open wounds and the eyes were blacked out, but he was still looking at dead bodies, and he forced himself to pause after a minute and look elsewhere, out the window into the eerie darkness of the morning, into the void of the TV. He pushed himself to look again, the first one of Chantelle, her body turned to face the strip mall's defaced facade, the next one of her rolled onto her back. A thin gold chain curled under her chin, a little cross connected to the bottom. The next picture showed Venture's left arm tucked beneath her hip, her chin dipped to her chest. And another necklace, another cross. He closed the message, blackened the screen, set the phone on the table, and buried his face back into the pillow.

Blake always considered that his ability to truly see inside himself was a trait not everyone possessed. He pored over his thoughts, reviewed what he said and how it affected people. Above all else, he wanted to understand something about himself and bridge the way he lived with the way he thought he wanted to be. And he knew he wasn't there, he'd gone off track a while ago and needed a way back.

He soon emerged with a renewed energy for the regular banalities of life he normally eschewed. Grabbed all the dirty clothes from the floor, took them to the garage and put them in the second-hand washing machine he'd hooked up after he moved back home and realized he didn't want to lug his clothes across the yard and into his mom's basement every time he needed to clean. Tossed on a hoodie and windbreaker and pulled on heavy boots, pushed a snow shovel up and down and across the sidewalks and driveway, brought the empty garbage can back from the road and wheeled it to the back of the house, brushed the flurries from the windshield of his mom's CR-V, took the newspaper from the plastic rectangle hanging below the mailbox and set it just inside the back door. A collection of surprises Mariana was sure to gawp at, but he didn't want to stop. Opened the computer and blitzed through his assignment, turned it in two days early, signed up for a shift at the fulfillment center later in the week, analyzed his credit card statement and checking account balance and other bills and plotted a schedule to get his Capital One debt to zero by the end of spring. Before lunch he grunted through dozens of sit-ups, three sets of pushups, stretches, mountain climbers, squats with an old dumbbell, even found the wrist roller he'd fashioned from a 10-lb. barbell plate and a plastic tube and turned it over and over until his arms gave out and he collapsed on the carpet, heaving satisfied sighs through gulps of ice water.

The anxiousness and pain of what was to come settled his brief euphoria. Amos needed to know about the cross, about the women in Louisville, and Blake realized his reticence about telling his brother-in-law was not about Tyner, but about being seen as a snitch, someone who runs to authority figures to tell on someone, even he knew enough not to be seen like that. But the time to open his mouth, he knew, had come.

Chapter 11

They met at the Diamond Grill and Lounge, not one of Blake's favorites, he rarely frequented restaurants for his drinks, preferring not to pay $12 for cocktails or $8 for beers, but Amos insisted so he could bring Landa dinner home with him. Blake commandeered a tall bar table and ordered Very Old Barton with ginger ale and lime, sat back and watched the diners, most of them older or middle-aged or just past the age of caring about impressing others with their clothing or demeanor. Lots of polos cinched all the way to the top, checked button-downs, women in formless slacks and big chunky sweaters. Lots of white people.

Amos strolled in one minute past seven, in full uniform, except the hat, and shook Blake's hand firmly, the kind of guy who believed in strong handshakes as the true measure of another man's worth. The server, a short, buxom brunette with a nose ring, ambled over with menus and placed them on the table, chirping, "What can I get started for you?" before Amos had a chance to look things over. He asked for ice water and folded his hands together on the wooden table, stared across at Blake for a few seconds.

"So wwwwhat's up. You said you nnnnnneeded to talk about something important."

"Yeah, yeah I do." He took a sip of the bourbon, the ginger ale too weak to diminish the burn much, and swallowed. "I appreciate you getting those photos to me."

"Well, normally I wouldn't, but you've at lllllleast got some medical training, and it's nothing to do with any of our ccccccases. So." A noise from the kitchen interrupted them, metal slamming into metal, and Amos turned the pages of the menu looking for an option for dinner.

"Actually, it does."

"Wwwwhat do you mean? Those were all gggggggirls in Louisville, black girls, strippers, we don't have anything like that over hhhhhhhere."

"I saw something that, well, it bothered me, about the pictures, the women. They either wore necklaces with a cross, or had a cross tattoo."

"So?"

"Jessie didn't have a cross on her necklace. Tyner bought it for her, just a plain gold chain. But I saw the pictures. I saw her wearing a cross."

"What? Whoooo showed you the pictures?"

"I have no idea. They came from a number I didn't recognize, two numbers, actually, told me to look at the photos and then delete them and keep my mouth shut. But once I saw the cross I got curious, I knew something was up, and that's why I asked you to send the pics of the Louisville women."

"That's nothing. She could have gotten that cross anytime, from anywhere, or anyone."

"No, I checked all the pictures I could find online, hundreds of them, not a single cross in any one. And the latest shot was uploaded on New Year's Eve, two weeks before she died, and there was nothing. I've known her for years and never saw her wearing that. You can ask anyone who knows her, even Landa."

"OK, OK. Hang on," he said, took a drink of water, then waved over the server and asked for a draft beer, preferably one without hops. "Jessie never wore a ccccccccross, ever. Someone you don't know sends you phhhhhhhotos of the bodies. And you spot a cross on her in one of those photos."

"I know, it's weird, and I didn't want to say anything, but once I found out about the other girls, I knew I had to tell you."

The beer arrived, Amos held it tenderly in his right hand and pointed at the menu with his left as he ordered food to go, salmon and blueberry sauce with a side of peas and risotto for Landa, pork chops with bacon and apples and the cheese grits for him. Blake held up his empty glass, indicating a second, and the server sauntered away with a little smile for one of them. At the end of the bar, two women, a blonde and a redhead, sat with drinks, one pink, the other brown with some kind of fruit inside.

"I don't know what you think I can ddddddo with this information. No one will care about the other girls, and this cross thing is some second-hand, hearsay shit I couldn't tell any other cop about, let anyone my bbbbboss."

"Come on, this isn't bullshit from some nut watching the news. I know her, I know that necklace, and I know something isn't right."

Amos took a sip of his beer, a small one, and Blake watched, realizing he'd never seen his brother-in-law drunk, even slightly tipsy, in all the years Landa had been with him. Blake had even been to a barbecue for the Amos family reunion a couple of years earlier, there were buckets of Heineken and Corona and bottles of brown liquor and liters of white wine everywhere, plates of food handed from person to person, music blasting from an impressive sound system a few cousins had hooked up, hours of dancing, talking, laughing, eating, drinking, and Amos had remained as docile and nonchalant as ever.

"Look, there's nnnnno way I can just bring this up. I have to find a way to make this seem like a nnnnnnatural part of the investigation." Blake tried to nod sympathetically but stopped, he didn't want Amos to think he approved of the by-the-book cop tactic he was receiving. He brought the glass of bourbon to his lips and made eye contact with one of the women drinking at the end of the bar. The redhead. Looked similar to the redhead he'd seen before, at the crime scene and after the funeral, but he'd never gotten a good look at her and couldn't really be certain, though he wanted to believe it was really her. They looked at one another, without expression, and Blake contemplated the marvelous coincidence that seemed to bring them together at the same place on the same night.

"Hey, do what you need to do so you don't get in trouble, but don't ignore this, please." He drained the rest of his bourbon as the takeout arrived at the table, and Blake dropped some cash on the table to cover his drinks. "I'm not trying to cause any trouble, but I can't not tell you what I found. This is serious, man. Jessie and those kids didn't just die. I think they were murdered."

Outside, Blake stood several steps away from the restaurant with his hands in his coat, shivering against the wind pressing in from the river. After a few minutes Amos left, turned in the other direction, and Blake scanned the amount of cash he had remaining, went back inside, pulled up to the bar a couple of seats away from the two women. With a heavy finger in the air he got the bartender's attention, asked for Basil Hayden, neat, with a small glass of ice cubes on the side. The blonde was closest to him but sat at an angle, her left side turned toward the redhead, who could see Blake quite clearly. After bringing the Basil, the bartender topped off the redhead's glass with some kind of whiskey in a funny-shaped bottle, one Blake didn't recognize.

"Excuse me," he said after a few seconds, and the redhead looked at him with big, open brown eyes. "What did he give you there? Is that rye?"

"Uh huh, a double rye from High West. It's got a good balance between spicy and sweet."

"Oh, like a bar of chocolate with cayenne pepper," he said with a grin.

"Yeah, I guess that's sort of apt. Although this doesn't come close to either of those designations." The blonde pushed her seat back and announced she was headed to the bathroom, and Blake got a closer look at the redhead. Jeans. Chuck Taylor's. A red blouse. And a leather jacket.

"What's your name? Are you new to Troy?"

"It's Lena. And yes, kind of, I moved here at the end of the summer."

"Wow, I didn't realize people like you were moving to Troy," he said, in the most mildly flirtatious voice he could muster, then cocked his head a little and gave her a quizzical look. "I know this sounds obvious and clichéd, so forgive me, but do we know each other? I swear I've seen you somewhere recently."

Lena returned the same searching look, and Blake could sense not only that she was trying to place him, to see if she recognized him, but the flash of attraction as she realized what he looked like up close. He knew the deal, women were into him on a basic, superficial level, there were never any questions about his multiracial makeup, his heritage, his hair, his color, his nose, the perceived advantages and disadvantages of his skin. All he had to do was smile, reveal the twin dimples on his cheeks, bat the long lashes that had made people swoon since he was a kid and show off his inexplicable green eyes, run a hand through the light brown curls that he sometimes let grow just a little long, and shake hands tenderly, the pale-brown tone of his arms and face enough to cause little giggles of nervousness and excitement.

Tyner might have been the basketball star, and dealt with the requisite attention based on his outsized talent and fame, but Blake drew the kind of attention reserved for a select few. He was genuinely handsome, attractive, able to halt girls in their tracks and cause fits of discomfort with a simple glance and grin.

"You know what, I probably have seen you, but if so, there's nothing about you I remember."

"Really? Nothing at all? Cause you see guys like me all the time around here, I assume."

"Well, no. Just that," she paused, started to laugh at the absurdity of where the conversation had taken, and took a drink. "And what's your name, so I won't forget who you are."

"Blake Prince. Let me guess, you like good food, good drinks, a good laugh, and a good story. The same as me."

"Not sure about that. Looks like you were drinking bottom shelf most of the night until just now."

"True, but I usually spring for better when I have the money. And shelf placement isn't always indicative of quality."

"You're all about the quality, right?"

"Of course," he said, and tilted his eyes up and down her ever so slightly, not in a skeevy way, but enough for her to notice . "I know it when I see it. And taste it."

The charged repartee continued until the blonde, who was introduced as Julie, came back from the bathroom, and Blake peeled away for a few minutes to finish his drink, use the bathroom, and prepare to dive back into the moment with Lena.

When he got back the women were shoving cards into bags and scrawling signatures on receipts, leaving him with not much time to formulate the necessary words to catapult their brief flirtation into something more.

"Before you take off, maybe we can figure this out sometime."

"Figure what out?" Lena asked with a little nod, her red hair spilling past the leather on her shoulder.

"This. Us. Where to meet, what to do."

"Oh, I see."

"So what's your preference for the next step? Text, call, Gchat, swipe, email?"

She lifted up her phone, also encased in leather, and said, "Text is good. Gives me a chance to decide if I want to respond to what you have to say," before reciting seven numbers, the area code unfamiliar to Blake.

"There it is," he said, smiled and started to back away as his phone buzzed in his pocket. "The start of something." A little wave, a turn, and he was outside and down the block in a matter of seconds.

The clothes were in a pile, his olive slacks, navy blue t-shirt emblazoned with the Vaqueros de Bayamón logo, the pro team in Puerto Rico that Tyner had briefly played for, black jacket, black boxer briefs, and the gray loafers he'd been wearing for more than four years. A few feet from the bed, near the heavy maroon drapes, on top of a thick Persian rug decorated with, as far as he could see in the dim light, a scene featuring Tigers attacking some kind of bird. He lay on his side, awake, looking at a gold-framed portrait of a formally-dressed woman with dark hair piled atop her head. The room, like the others, was decorated to the nines, a showcase for how money could be spent in frivolous ways.

A rustle next to him made him shift to his back, and he saw that Clarke was coming out of her post-coital slumber. Her hair looked sharp and tactile on the pillow, her breasts visible as the heavy comforter had slid down to her abdomen. Blake stared for a moment, then lifted himself out of the bed to retrieve his clothes.

"Where are you going?" Clarke half-whispered, and Blake slid on his underwear before turning to her.

"I gotta go to the bathroom. I'll be right back."

"You're leaving, aren't you?"

"Just going to the bathroom, like I said."

"You're supposed to stay with me until I'm ready for you to go." Her pouty eyes barely resonated in the semi-darkness, and he ran his hand over his chest for a moment, trying to remember some of the rules she'd laid out for them when he first ventured to the little guest house outside the mansion. She demanded he never use her real name, never call her, never text her unless she texted him first, never show up unannounced, never invite himself over, never talk to her if he saw her out in public, never acknowledge any member of her family, and never stay longer than she asked him to. He'd agreed to all the rules because, well, it was Clarke. A legendary beauty that Blake vividly recalled when he was just a freshman, everyone talked about her at TCHS, all the older guys, all the ball players, the black guys and even the white boys salivated over her body, her unparalleled beauty, she was exotic before anyone knew what that meant.

Blake knew, he didn't need to see anyone in her family to know she was mixed just like him, and he took notice and kept track of every interested party and boyfriend that crossed her path, even though she was a senior and most of what he knew came second- and third-hand. By the time he graduated, her marriage to an older, rich white man was common knowledge, and photos of her engagement party, bridal shower, wedding, and reception were splashed all over the paper and even some of the Louisville lifestyle magazines.

"I know, but I have work tomorrow, I need to get some sleep, I can't just lay here all night." Without looking back he pulled on the rest of his clothes, unsure if his tone or his behavior was causing more of a problem, but for once he didn't care about her reaction. She remained silent as he tied his shoes and tugged his arms through the coat sleeves, and when he looked back she'd shoved the comforter all the way to her feet, every inch of her body naked and exposed to the slight chill of the room. He took one last look as she pulled her knees up to her chin, then walked out, his coat unzipped, his head uncovered, unconcerned with the freezing temperatures and the icy walkway and crunchy grass as he made his way through the yard to his car.

The music filtered quietly out of the speakers, Teddy Pendergrass' swooping, aching baritone over the strings and the soft backing vocals of the Blue Notes lamenting the same issues magnified in every R&B and soul song. A lone streetlight from a few hundred yards away threw an artificial block of light on the asphalt as he parked near his apartment, just enough for him to see as he stepped gingerly to the doorway. Not a sound, nothing from any neighbors, no pets, no other cars, no cargo planes roaring overhead to the shipping hub across the river, and he complied with the silence by slipping inside without making any noise. Immediately, with no hesitation and no delay, he stripped off his clothes and stepped into the shower, didn't even wait for the tiny, hard rivulets to reach their max temperature before plunging his face into the spray. Tumbled into bed without a drink, movie, show, or random dive into YouTube clips.

He tried to sleep but his brain went wild, thoughts of three women running rampant, Jessie and Clarke and Lena. Clarke was done, she wanted nothing to do with him after he bailed on her, and Blake figured their thing had run its course. Lena, brand-new, exciting, mysterious, his heart and his body trying to keep up with the images of her in his mind. And Jessie. Maybe he'd loved her all along, from the time he first saw her with Tyner, and his obsession with her death was more about handling his misplaced affection than about mourning the tragedy of her and her kids.

A scream, a real one, pierced his subconscious a few hours later, then again, and he bolted up, looked out the window at the street, grabbed sweatpants and a hoodie and clopped down the stairs and into the yard. Another scream, a blubbering wail, he turned to the neighbor's fence. And saw nothing but blood.

The cold didn't bother him, it never had, and he sat quietly in his truck and watched. It seemed stupid and dangerous to continue what he was doing, but it also felt wrong to stop. He chewed the inside of his cheeks and kept his eyes on the light above, but the noise gnawed at him, the incessant noise. The harping and the critiques. The voice that never stopped. He stepped out of the truck, the light missed him, and he moved slowly into the darkness.

Chapter 12

The blood ate into the snow in jagged, angry shapes, dark red in some spots, almost pink in others. Blake stood next to the wooden fence and watched his neighbor, a short, squat, pale woman of around 50 with exceptionally short hair and large black glasses, hold her face in her hands and continue to weep loudly, though the screams had ended. The Malamute lay at her feet, most of its head gone, nearly disintegrated from an endless number of blows from a spattered shovel propped against a mimosa tree nearby. A pool of blood glimmered where the muzzle and brains and skull and ears had once been, bits of fur were strewn around the snow-covered yard, and spurts of red jutted up the sides of the fence opposite Blake.

After a minute Mariana came out of the house, saw Blake, saw the scene, and let out a gasp of astonishment. He was unaccustomed to his mom displaying much in the way of emotion, her stoicism extended to most circumstances in their lives, but seeing animals hurt always jarred something loose in her, and she covered her mouth with one hand and put the other gently on Blake's arm. "What happened? What in the world- who would do this?"

"I don't know," he said quietly, and put an arm around her shoulders to keep her calm. The family only raised one dog while he and Landa were growing up, Beau, a spunky little black-and-white spaniel mix who could play fetch for hours, never had a single accident in the house, and slept soundly, night after night, in a little dog bed in Landa's room. But Beau escaped the yard one night when the whole family was at one of Tyner's basketball games, and they came home to him panting and whimpering and crawling along his belly on the sidewalk out front, dazed and oblivious to everyone calling his name, and by the end of the night Mariana and Nelson made the painful call to put him down after the vet said he'd fractured multiple vertebrae, most likely from being hit by a car. Mariana kept Beau's ashes in a simple little wooden box on her dresser, and though she never chastised either of the kids for leaving the gate open and leading, unintentionally, to the dog's death, Blake suspected she'd always wanted to blame one of them for what happened, to have an explanation and to get the closure she needed.

"Gloria, I'm so sorry," Mariana said, then turned and walked back to her house, shouting over her shoulder, "I'm calling the police right now!"

"Miss Doherty, is there anything I can do? Ma'am?" Blake asked, hoping the answer was no, as much as the gruesomeness in front of him turned his stomach, he was not all that unhappy that the Malamute would no longer be such a consistent pain in the ass.

"No, honey, no," she sputtered through her fingers, then started to speak softly, her breathy voice a hearty, audible whisper. "Up in heaven, high above, today you sit with the angels. You knew when I was happy, you knew when I was sad, you became a part of me, you woke my soul, and I will love you to the very end. God will ease my heart, and He will welcome you with open arms. My love, my friend, my Ambrose, goodbye. Amen."

Blake stood awkwardly, unsure how to offer words of comfort. He had always been bad at that aspect of life, had failed to do anything substantial for a teenaged Landa when their father died, never engaged in a real, painful conversation with his mother, didn't seem to know how to speak, didn't have the kind of spirituality or grace that would lead him to the kinds of answers he could convey to those suffering around him.

His mom came out with the black house phone up to her ear, her accent thickening mid-conversation as she tried to relay the horrors to whomever was listening on the other end. Eventually she was able to explain it all, told Blake to go inside and make coffee, and when he returned with a pair of travel mugs for the two women, a squad car was idling in front of his Camry and two officers were getting out. They asked questions, took pictures with their cell phones, performed a cursory search of the yard and street before the Animal Services team arrived. One of the cops asked Blake if he'd seen or heard anything, knew of anyone with a vendetta against Miss Doherty, and he could only shake his head and say no.

The cleanup would start soon, Blake knew, and he wanted to avoid seeing any more of the unholy scene, and walked away after one of the newly arrived workers scraped one of the dog's eyes off the fence. The smell of the coffee he'd brewed finally stirred some hunger pangs, and he went upstairs found a microwavable oatmeal package deep in his cupboard, stirred in milk and honey and a few almonds, went to his computer and posted about the dog, noting that his dislike of the animal was not mean-spirited and he was horrified at what happened.

Nothing else called to him, nothing inspired him, he had no interest in the news or Tyner or Jessie or work, and he didn't feel it was appropriate to wile away minutes and hours on the usual nonsense. He stood up and walked around the apartment for a minute or two, his eyes scanning the meager possessions he'd brought out of his childhood room and lugged from undergrad to med school and back to the apartment. A record player sat on a small table in the corner, a Pioneer direct-drive turntable that had belonged to Nelson. His dad's records were shoved under the table, mostly jazz and gospel music that Blake had never been interested in despite his professed love for R&B and soul, and he knelt down and fingered the scuffed cardboard sleeves, flipped past the faces of names of legends he had never really listened to, stopped at one that featured a man with his eyes slightly closed, sitting at a piano with a massive double bass leaning against the wall behind him. *Charles Mingus Presents Charles Mingus*, it read, and he lifted the vinyl out and placed it on the turntable, then realized the player wasn't hooked up to a receiver or speakers. Wires dangled from behind the table, and he felt for them and analyzed them in his hands, remembered the extra-long cord he'd bought to extend to the equipment under his TV, connected the audio cables, found the right input setting, and dropped the needle on the black vinyl. A smoky, vibrant voice began making announcements to the audience before throbbing acoustic bass, drums, and jittery horns started up. It wasn't really his thing, his style of music, but he let it play and sat back down at the computer and let the jaunty horns and skittering drums settle over him.

Then a trumpet, joined by a pair of raspy voices that belted out, "Oh Lord, don't let 'em shoot us, oh Lord, don't let 'em stab us!" The call-and-response that followed, the rousing voices and chunky rhythm and bracing stabs of sax and trumpet, made him halt his typing and searching. A sense of spirituality seemed to hover over him, though he'd never believed in anything resembling Christianity and laughed, inside, at those who put all of their hopes and wishes and prayers into something they couldn't see or touch. But there seemed to be an authenticity to the emotion woven through the music, and Blake closed his eyes, made himself feel everything that Mingus and Dolphy and Richmond and Curson were pouring into their songs.

The song ended, the vinyl turned and turned without stopping, popping and crackling on the black plastic turntable. He thought of something, the middle of nowhere, the cold, the snow, the creek, and he got dressed, got into the Camry, and drove.

St. Aureus beckoned, and Blake headed there in the bright gray daylight, for some reason compelled to listen to George Clinton's craziness from the 70s, and bobbed his head along to the group of acid-dropping funk-freaks slurring and groaning, "There's been a change, and it's oh so plain to see." He hadn't realized, for some many years, the entirety of his life, really, that St. Aureus was not just a church, but a monastery and theological school run by Cistercian monks and nuns. The number of faculty and staff and students and brothers and sisters who lived there seemed impossible to determine, there was no real way to know which buildings were dorms or apartments or even houses. There were no impediments on any of the campus roads, which allowed Blake to drive anywhere he wanted, and he puttered around for 10 minutes looking at various structures and trying to determine what had brought Jessie there that morning.

The spot where he'd parked before was empty, the police tape gone, nothing to indicate the horrors that had taken place there, and he kept driving, looped back around and took a different path, this time finding a small parking lot marked with a large wooden sign carved with the words, "The Witness Path." He slid into a space, the car angled slightly, and got out, saw that a series of stones and a walkway led into the woods, and he followed the markers, his old running shoes crunching against the packed snow. Without the heavy canopy of leaves surrounding, he was able to take in the various paths looping through the woods, the small wooden bridges built over trickles of water that eventually fed into the creek, large wooden crosses staked along different parts of the path, wooden benches tucked into cozy corners, and the undulating hills of the St. Aureus campus.

A lone set of footprints caught his attention, and he tracked them down a path and around a large white boulder that seemed to grow out of the earth. Small feet, he thought, and slowed his pace, kept his eyes down and his hands in the pockets of his red OSU hoodie. The path wound up a little, started to narrow, and he saw a person ahead of him, standing in front of a cluster of stones about five feet high and topped by an arch. Candles lit the interior, which contained a small figurine of a robed man, a monk, presumably, posed serenely. He stopped 15 or 20 feet away, noticed the red hair, and scraped his foot along the ground to get her attention.

She turned swiftly, her eyes large with surprise but not alarm or fear, and her mouth widened in a smile. "Wow. Blake, what are you doing here?"

"Hey there," he said with a grin. "Walking, exploring, freezing."

"Really? It's not that bad today," she said with a little grin, and Blake noticed her lack of heavy winter clothing, no hat or gloves or thick boots.

"Twenty degrees and snow isn't that bad?"

"Not for me, I'm from Wisconsin, this is just a basic winter day."

"And you head to the most remote place you can think of on a basic day, I suppose."

"I like to walk to clear my head, relax, and it's always better to do it where it's quiet, with minimal distractions."

"Am I a distraction?"

"No, a little company is fine."

He moved closer to her and peered in at the statue, then turned to face her. "What is this, some kind of shrine?"

"Sort of, it's a grotto dedicated to St. Bernard of Clairvaux, the sign says he was a French abbot and an early leader of the Order of Cistercians."

"The what? I thought this place was for monks or friars or something."

"It is, the Cistercians are the White Monks, kind of an offshoot of the Benedictines."

"Oh, ok. So you know the differences between all of them."

"No, not all, I grew up Catholic, so I know of the Benedictines and Franciscans and Dominicans and Trappists and Capuchins and Augustinians. But honestly, I had never heard of Cistercians before I moved here, and there are so many different monastic orders and different kinds of friars and whatnot." She shifted in the snow and waved her hand toward the main campus. "They all basically believe in an ascetic and cloistered life dedicated to the state of perfection and the ideals of poverty, chastity, and obedience. Different names and communities and rules, but that's about it."

They both moved away from the grotto and took the path that led toward one of the small bridges. She'd moved to Troy for her internal medicine residency at Hudson Memorial Health, she told him, and had just completed her internship year and passed the final medical licensure exam. Blake listened wistfully, not intending to reveal too much about his own brush with graduate school, instead focusing on her life and her interests outside of the hospital, which were severely limited by the time constraints of being a rookie doctor.

What he could do, though, was issue compliments. They were subtle, he knew not to go too hard on a woman like Lena so early, but simple, flattering comments were always appreciated. "I like that wrap. It makes your hair look great." "That sweater is cool, I like the wide collar." "Your family must be so proud of your accomplishments." "Thanks for explaining the monks to me, you're good at breaking things down." "Growing up in the cold gave you those pretty rosy cheeks all the time, I bet." She smiled at them all, didn't say much beyond thanks and thank you, but the correct effect had been achieved.

"Well, I'm parked over there," she said as they reached the end of the path, and he could see a different lot than the one he'd parked his Camry, larger and closer to one of the administrative buildings. "Thanks for walking with me."

"Sure, I hope I didn't disturb your peaceful sojourn too much."

"Of course not, I was just so surprised to see you up here. I didn't realize you spent time at places like this."

"I never did, until a few days ago. After the, you know, the family was found, I came to see the creek, the church, everything." He stopped, looked down at his feet, the subject matter suddenly heavy, and he hated that he'd sucked the coy tone out of the conversation so suddenly. "I knew Jessie, I knew the kids. Tyner is, he was one of my best friends."

"Oh my goodness, I'm so sorry. I had no idea."

"Yeah, it's been a rough time lately. I just wish I could figure out what happened, you know, and make sure people stop looking at Tyner like he did something. He loved those kids, he's not some monster who would hurt them, no matter what was going down between him and Jessie."

"No, of course not." She lifted her head a little, the brown of her eyes light and dusty in the piercing dullness of the early afternoon. "I never said anything before, I didn't think about it until now. But I saw the family at the hospital. I mean, they brought them to the Hud that morning, I was working, and there was a thought, briefly, that maybe they could revive one of the kids, so they brought them all in, but of course it was too late. And the coroner came in and handled everything, but I was haunted by those kids for a while. Still am, really."

"Father, father, it's for the kids, any and everything I did. Please, please don't judge me too strong," Blake whispered to himself, looking back at the woods and the faint outline of the creek that appeared behind the treeline. "Lord knows I meant no wrong."

"What's that?"

"Huh?"

"What's that you were saying? Some kind of prayer?"

"Oh," he mumbled, and rearranged his gaze to take in all of Lena. "Sorry, no it's from a song. When you just said that about the kids and how you felt, it just came to my mind."

"I see." She didn't ask anything else and he didn't offer up more, and they kept moving out of the woods.

"Well, this has definitely conjured some feelings I hadn't planned on, but maybe we can plan something a little more fun. Check out someplace unique in town to get dinner or lunch or whatever your schedule can accommodate."

"Unique is good, I've only seen common since I've been here. Can I let you know a day that works for me? Maybe text you later?"

"Yeah, anytime." Without hesitating he leaned toward her for a hug, nothing too intense but enough to let her know he was not shy to make a move or touch her. The contact lasted more than a friend hug, and he watched her walk away with a little smile and a little flutter in his stomach.

And watched her get into a small black Volkswagen.

Leaving and going. That was always an issue, and he struggled with the idea that no one believed as much as he did and that all of the protocols needed to be tightened. His whole life had been spent there, he'd been shaped by the words, the lands, the service, and the man who led him in every possible way. At times he'd tried to persuade the others to change, to become, totally and completely, what had been taught and preached for so long. Most obeyed; some did not.

The body that disappeared and was found in the 80s caused a major problem, and new rules were put in place to prevent it from occurring again. But it had happened, it was happening, and he didn't know if things would continue as they had been, how they sang their songs and talked and lived within a world of their own making. The words weren't enough, not anymore, he had listened his whole life, faced criticisms and critiques unlike any other, and it was time for it all to change, to end.

They left, and he did not follow. He knew where they were going. And he had his own task to take care of.

Chapter 13

Amos emailed him, a first, and Blake had to double-check the address to make sure it wasn't spam hitting his inbox. A link to an article, the only thing in the message, and he clicked it immediately before realizing it was a news story from one of the Louisville TV stations. Another dead body, another young black woman, Destiny Baxter, this time her body found near the railroad tracks behind a church close to Iroquois Park on the city's southwest side. But the article featured a small picture likely pulled from a social media account, the victim posed in front of a small, brick house, her outfit all pink, large oval sunglasses perched atop her curly black hair, a large brown purse hanging from her left hand, a thin, almost bemused smile on her face. And the sparkle of a little gold earring A cross.

He wrote back to Amos, asking if there was something to his notion, his theory, but didn't get a response. No other news outlet had coverage of the death, and he bookmarked the story in a folder he'd titled Tyner. A rumbling caught his attention, he looked out the window and saw a white pickup with an empty trailer attached, walked downstairs in his shorts and long-sleeve shirt and sandals, and covered his ears at the sound of a small excavator digging through the frozen soil and rock of Miss Doherty's backyard. She stood quietly on the concrete porch 20 feet away, wearing a heavy black parka and sweatpants, her arms folded and face contorted into a mask of despair and anger. The machine scooped and dumped the detritus off to the side and left a deep, rectangular hole in the middle of the yard, and after a few minutes the excavator rolled back to the truck and onto the trailer, the driver went to Mrs. Doherty and gave her a slip of paper. As Blake looked over the yard, he noticed a few spots of blood still visible in the snow, but the shovel was gone, and a large round stone was leaning against the fence, the name Ambrose imprinted atop a large pair of paw prints.

The little blue light on his phone blinked at him, and he grabbed for it, expecting an answer or something from Amos. But the name Tyner flashed at him, and a short message: "When are we getting together??"

The feeling, immediately, in his stomach, in his chest, was overwhelming and tense and terrifying. They hadn't been alone together in so long, hadn't even provided each other with the basics of friendship, and Blake knew if they got together that Tyner would pretend that no time at all had passed, that their lives had continued along the same path and trajectory and they were still boys like they'd been back in the day.

"Hey, good to hear from you. I know a lot has happened and you probably have a lot on your mind, just tell me when and where."

"Let's do this weekend, Saturday if that's cool with you, we're having a small family service on Friday to remember the kids and Jessie. Nine at the Mill good?"

"Yeah, see you then." He wanted to say more, add more of a sympathetic vibe, but his fingers just stopped and he knew it was best to just wait and talk in person. The afternoon sun peeked brightly through the moat of clouds that seemed to have permanently settled over the region in recent weeks, and Blake opened his curtains and worked without needing to turn on the little touch lamp he kept near his desk. An automated email burst into his work folder, the fulfillment center bots warning him that if he didn't work another shift in the next week he'd be terminated instantly. He didn't care, decided right then and there his previous shift at the stifling, mind-numbing warehouse was his last. He had started to quietly chip away at his life, and spending any more time on tasks and people that didn't matter would only halt the progress he'd made.

The next couple of days showed that he was still capable of the kind of focus he'd shown to during his time in college, when he'd set an alarm and awake to the first rays of the sun and stretch and get dressed and prepare for the day and attack every class, assignment, chapter, lab, meeting, email, phone call, jog, get-together, party, date, and intimate moment with a clarity and ferocity he knew would serve him well as a successful doctor. He started to eat much better, too, eliminated the sweet, processed crap that had saddled him with an additional 10 pounds, and though he seemed unable or unwilling to stop having a few drinks at night, he stopped reaching the indelicate point of inebriation that led to inconsistent memories and numb feelings.

Lena called him, too, and their amiable, friendly, suggestive banter continued, her voice somehow more mellifluous over the phone, and Blake found himself fantasizing about her as they made plans to meet on Monday night, her next available evening. He'd never kissed or touched a redhead before, he'd actually had sex with just three white women in his life, shocking, he thought, when he counted in his head and came up with nearly 20 women total. Most of them were fellow light-brights, girls with one black and one white parent, or a dad or mom with some mixed heritage of their own, leaving their daughters with the kind of deliciously warm, sandy color that Blake sought over and over. But Lena projected the kind of confidence he'd always craved, a woman so comfortable with her talent and her abilities and her personality and her looks that she'd stay the same no matter how long the relationship progressed, she'd never compromise her own happiness, a trait he longed for not only in a woman, but in himself.

Saturday came, Blake still hadn't heard back from Amos about the idea that the deaths in Louisville and Jessie's family were somehow connected, and he considered that the initial email was just to distract him and lead him to a place of wondering and worrying about something so big that nothing could possibly come of it. Maybe there was some truth to that, and maybe the whole thing was in his head, the cross could have been Jessie's, she could have gotten it on her own or from someone else and worn it that day, and it was likely no one would ever take the idea of some dead black girls seriously, let alone that they were related to the tragedy of a white woman from Indiana.

Dressing to meet Tyner always proved problematic, he knew he couldn't play it down because of the high probability of running into people out in public, but his fashion choices were limited by his budget, and he never seemed to have the time or keen, critical eye to know what to buy that would look sharp and wouldn't trouble his thin checking account or weary credit score. So he tended to keep his looks basic, jeans and solid colors and white Original Penguins and some jackets that looked expensive. Tyner was one of those guys who always looked great, who walked out of his house every day in praise-worthy looks no matter where he was headed and no matter the occasion, he'd mastered relaxed, natural, easy, elegant, classic, elevated, and casual looks that made him stand out in Troy and Louisville and Indianapolis and everywhere in between.

Blake arrived a few minutes late but before Tyner, asked for a booth and sat with his back to the wall and his eyes scanning the front door. They always met at the Mill but usually grabbed seats at the bar, drinks and conversation never necessitated a whole table, but that night Blake felt the need for more privacy. The noise level hovered just below a din as he waited and sipped a vanilla ale from one of the Louisville breweries, but it dropped to an enthralled hush as soon as Tyner entered. Eyes followed, talk stopped, four white guys at the bar craned their necks and followed his every move, and the only two black guys in the place, outside of the kitchen staff, became the focus of the room as Tyner folded his 6'5" frame into the booth.

"What's up, man, how've you been?" Tyner asked with a smile.

"I'm good, doing alright. How are you handling everything?"

"It's been crazy, honestly. Trying to get through all this, talking to people, talking to cops, family, insurance companies, reporters." He ran his hand across his face, over a scraggly beard that was at odds with the meticulous grooming he normally sported. It seemed patchy and uneven, like he had given up, but his hairline was perfect and he was wearing a long beige coat with heavy brown lapels and a chocolate shirt underneath and white pants. "Feels like I don't have a whole lot of people on my side right now. People blame me for what happened, even though no one knows what happened."

"What did happen? You were, like, gone, and your family went to that church campus and, I don't know, they just went away." The head on his ale had disappeared, and Blake lifted it to his mouth, stared into the creamy yellow liquid and regretted the demeanor he'd taken. He meant what he said, but he'd seen Tyner's fury unleashed before, on the court, in practices, and one time against a couple of rival fans who cornered him after a game, and the consequence of that anger usually resulted in blood spilled and Tyner quickly leaving the scene so he wouldn't get in trouble.

"Listen, me and Jessie had our problems, you know that. She got mad at me because I had business over in Louisville and just wanted to stay there instead of coming home at 1 in the morning all the damn time. Shit just got so old, all the arguing, my opinion never mattered about anything and she just shut everything down when I tried to tell her what I needed and what was best for me and for us." A waitress scooted up tentatively, her pad and pen already out, but Blake saw her and waved her away, not wanting an interruption to the heavy conversation. "I wasn't there at the house, and I don't know what she was up to, I don't know why they went to the woods and that damn creek, but if she was here I'd be be screaming at her to tell me why my kids had to get caught up in her bullshit and end up dead."

Blake covered his mouth, he could tell Tyner's raised ire was drawing some attention, not only from the gaggle of white guys at the bar but the older couples sitting nearby, their glasses of wine stopping mid-gulp and their forks resting on the edges of their plates with cuts of steak and chunks of pasta hanging on the tines. He tried to refocus Tyner, get him to recall memories of the kids and the time they spent together, which worked, especially when it came to his son, Georgy. "I couldn't wait to teach him the game, teach him how to be a man, make him better than me. I think about that shit all the time." The server finally found a chance to jump in and Tyner ordered ginger ale, grit cakes and a spinach salad loaded with chopped fried chicken, cheese, and pecans. Blake stuck with his beer, he'd eaten a sandwich and an apple before he left the apartment, and the mood at the table finally started to lighten.

"Anyway, man, I was wondering what you've been up to recently, if you've been working at night, going anywhere at all," Tyner said. "I met with my lawyer the other day, I'm not in any kind of trouble or anything, but we talked about a strategy going forward of making sure all the people in my life can speak to what I'm like, how I was with the kids, what I did with my time. And maybe, if you were free that night, you can say we were hanging out when everything happened."

Blake frowned behind his eyes, contemplating what he'd just heard. "I mean, I was with someone that night, but she won't want me to say anything about that. I went home later, woke up when my mom came and told me what happened. That's about it."

"OK, so there's not a problem, then."

"No, I guess not. But I can't lie about this kind of shit to the cops, it's too big."

"It ain't about lying, it's about making sure they can focus on the right things instead of worrying about me."

"It still seems, I don't know if wrong is the word, but like there's a big chance it can end up being a big problem. For me and for you." He looked down at his hands, they were pale and plain and starting to shake. "But if it comes up, I can say we hung out, watched a movie."

"OK, but say something specific, something I've seen, like *Iron Man* or *Avengers* or something."

"OK." Tyner seemed satisfied and started to twist leaves of spinach and pieces of chicken into his mouth while Blake sat back and held his beer. "Hey, let me ask you this. Cause I heard from someone that you were over in Louisville for a couple of days when Jessie was gone. Where were you, for real?"

"I had some shit to do, just stayed over there for a couple of days."

"Yeah, but who were you with?"

"Just a friend, someone who lets me crash and doesn't ask questions."

"A guy."

"A friend, man."

"People are saying it's a guy."

"I don't give a fuck what people are saying."

"Yeah, I get it, but if I'm talking to cops and whoever, they're gonna ask about that, that's what people are saying and I'll need an answer."

"Say whatever you want, that shit doesn't matter." His tone shifted to defiance, annoyance, and he reached in his pocket, yanked a wad of bills out, unfurled a pair of 20s and put them on the table. "I gotta go, thanks for meeting me and having my back. Stay safe, man." He got up and walked out, leaving Blake with a plate of half-eaten food and the cash. Another favor, another test of loyalty that Blake knew he needed to pass. He'd done it so many times, going all the way back to middle school when he carried a stolen Zippo lighter out of a convenience store, and the drive to the clinic in Indianapolis, and when he left school during a snowstorm and went to Philadelphia to take a drug test in Tyner's place. He'd given a lot and received hardly anything in return, other than an association with a locally famous basketball player, which was proving to be worth less and less as the years went on.

Blake added his cash to the table, signaled the waitress and smiled at her as he got up. Outside, he looked around for Tyner but didn't see him or his SUV. A rush of warm air hit him from behind and he turned to see the four white guys coming out of the restaurant, their breath steaming and their hands rubbing together and their eyes glassy and their laughter erupting.

"Where'd your friend go?" one of them slurred, and Blake shrugged in the general direction of the guys. Two of them turned and walked to the parking lot, while the other two, one in a white hat and the other, smaller one wearing a black windbreaker, tried to circle around him as he started to walk down the street.

"Don't know," he said, kept his head down and kept moving, the guys trailing slightly, their voices echoing off the brick walls of the buildings around them, mostly empty storefronts and businesses closed for the day and restaurants that had come and gone.

"That's the baby killer, isn't it, that black dude? Killed his whole family." The taller one said it, and Blake didn't respond. He'd dealt with guys like that before, overly aggressive white assholes hellbent on tormenting him because they suspected he was black and they really wanted to fuck with him. Stand up, stand tall, his dad used to tell him. Don't back down from no one, Tyner would say. Mariana always suggested he walk away and treat any sort of bully dismissively, like they didn't bother him and they didn't matter. His approach combined all the tactics he learned, especially because he'd been on the small side until his junior year of high school and needed to deal with guys trying to punk him. But he avoided fights, he avoided getting his ass kicked, and not just because he was friends with Tyner, he found a way to let those kinds of guys know he wasn't just a punching bag without putting up his fists.

"Why are you hanging out with that guy? You have something to do with that shit, boy?"

"That was an accident, no one had anything to do with it."

"Bullshit, he killed that girl and them kids, everyone knows it."

"Nah, nah man." He picked up the pace but they kept up for a half block, shouting and trying to draw him into a confrontation, but he resisted until one started tugging at his coat. "Hey, don't touch me."

"Oh, don't touch you, huh? Don't touch you?" A pair of hands shoved him in the back and he stumbled forward, nearly slipped on the slick sidewalk, and he put his hand on the nearest building to steady himself and turn around.

"Fuck you think you're doing?" Blake yelled, but the dam had been broken, and one of them threw a wild punch that he ducked. He backed away quickly with his hands up, tried to avoid the swings coming from multiple directions, but he tripped on the icy walkway and fell, his arm slammed into the brick building, and a scraggly fist connected under his left eye, snapped his head back a little and left him scrambling in the darkness, unable to make out anything but the shapes of his attackers. He ducked a punch at his head, stepped away from one headed toward his midsection, swung at the shadow in front of him and seemed to land against a scratchy, fleshy cheek, but then felt a deflating kick to the gut, a thick work boot slammed into his stomach, and he doubled over with his back against the wall. Then another hit, one more destructive blow against his skull, and warm, sticky blood drizzled down the side of his head, into his ear, down his neck and onto his chest. He wobbled, lurched, went limp. And closed his eyes for good.

Chapter 14

Looking for the answer, looking for the road, looking for an ending, and instead he found the cold, gritty expanse of the sidewalk against his face. Lights flashed and went away and he opened his eyes as best he could. A hand touched his shoulder and he jerked away, sat up and tried to find the face, pressed his fingers and palms down to lift himself up and flinched against the spiky, frozen concrete.

"You alright buddy?" the voice asked, and he recognized the tone and tenor of a cop right away.

"I don't know. Guess so."

"What happened? We got a call that said some guys were running away from an altercation here on Central Ave. That you?"

"Yeah, a couple of guys followed me out of the Mill and went off, ran me down and took a few swings." Blake blinked away the fuzzy circles in his eyes, winced as he felt the side of his head, looked around and saw a small chunk of black plastic on the ground with a spot of red on it.

"Who was it that you got in a fight with?"

"It wasn't a fight," he said and stood up with a grunt, the cop did the same and they looked at each other. "They followed me down the street, one of them pushed me and I bumped into the wall, they started swinging and kicking and one of them must have hit me with a phone."

"OK. You said they were at the Mill and followed you, was there anything that happened there?"

"No, they were in the bar area, I was sitting at a booth. With a friend. He left, then I came out and started to walk home." He reached down, grabbed a handful of snow and pressed it to his head, realized the blood hadn't stopped running when he saw the crimson slush fall out of his fingers. "I think I'm gonna need stitches. Do you think you can give me a ride to the hospital? I walked here."

"Sure. Can you tell me anything about the guys, a description, their names, anything?"

"Only thing I remember is one of them had on a UK hat, the other had a black jacket. White guys. They were sitting at one of the tables in the bar. Like I said, I was walking away so I didn't get too good a look at them."

"Sit tight, sir. I'll pop inside and see if the bartender or a waiter saw those guys. Here," the cop reached into his jacket and pulled out a wad of tissues, handed them to Blake, then walked down the block and inside the restaurant. The wad quickly turned to mush, and Blake tossed it to the ground and grabbed another scoop of snow, packed it firm, and held it to his head. The cop came out a few minutes later, motioned for Blake to follow, and the two got into an SUV emblazoned with Troy City Police logos and slogans. The drive to the hospital took less than five minutes, Blake walked in with the cop, spoke with a nurse at the registration desk, took a small cotton towel from her, and sat on a black vinyl chair holding the cloth to his head. A man came in right after him, told the triage nurse he might have the flu, and she asked him to sit and wait. Two women huddled in the corner of the room in comically thin clothes, their elbows and collar bones poking through t-shirts, their eyes large and unfocused. A Latino family sat near him, everyone silent except a sniffling little boy. What the hell am I doing here, Blake thought, and looked up at the TV hanging from the ceiling and watched aimlessly as celebrities laughed and guffawed playing some kind of silly game meant to evoke the nostalgia of the 70s.

"Mr. Prince," he heard, a nurse had poked her head out of the doorway leading to the rooms of the emergency department, and he followed, nodded to the cop still standing by the triage station and left his number for the cop to get in touch. The hallway stretched in front of him, the beeps of monitors and the squeak of Crocs and clogs and running shoes the only sounds as he trailed the nurse into a little room. She sat him down and began cleaning the wound while speaking gently and asking him where he lived, then another woman in scrubs joined in, a physician assistant who smiled brightly, probed his head, and lobbed a series of basic questions at him to assess whether he had a brain injury.

"How'd this happen?" the PA asked as her strong, determined fingers felt around the cut. He told the two women about the Mill and the idiots who'd attacked him, and the PA tsked and shook her head and lamented the state of things in Troy, then realized what he looked like, gave in and began to look deeper in his eyes.

"This cold is making people act all kinds of crazy," the nurse chimed in.

No residual dizziness or wooziness remained, his vision had returned, and the pain seemed isolated to the wound itself, and the PA asked the nurse to clean the area further so she could apply a topical anesthetic and close the laceration with surgical staples.

"Good thing I still have insurance, those staples aren't cheap" he muttered, and the PA nodded in agreement, then left with a smile to gather the supplies she needed.

"Blake?" A female voice echoed from the hall, and he swiveled on the exam table and saw Lena, her face creamy against the blue of her scrubs and her hair pulled back and held together with a thick black band.

"Hey," he said, trying his best not to seem too somber or flushed. "How's it going?"

"What are you doing here? What happened?"

"Ah, just some knuckleheads, they got a little feisty with me at the bar, I'm alright," he said and tried not to wince as the nurse rubbed the sore spot on his scalp with a briny solution.

"God, that's crazy. Who was it, did you know them or something?"

"No, no, I was hanging out, they were drunk and stupid, caught me outside, then ran away like a couple of punks. It's all good, seriously, it's not that bad. I've dealt with worse."

"I guess I'm not that surprised. I mean, I am, that it's you in here, but I've seen my share of these kinds of things since I've been here."

"Oh yeah, we definitely have a type here," he said with a laugh. "All you have to do is tell people you're from Troy City, and they know what's up ."

The PA returned with her equipment and looked oddly at Lena, but Blake said it was fine to have her inside. The procedure commenced and he said goodbye, giving a little wink to let her know that he'd be fine, and she left with a promise to call him the next day and see how he was doing. After 20 more minutes of discomfort his head had been stapled and he had a prescription for a mild painkiller, he thanked the nurse and the PA and thought about walking home, then remembered the disturbing cold outside, fumbled for his phone and saw that it was already 2 in the morning, too late to call his mom. He considered texting or calling Tyner but declined, checked his phone to see if a Lyft was nearby or had to come all the way from Louisville, then saw a sign in the lobby with the number of a local cab company, flicked through his small wad of cash, $25, enough for a ride, and he made the call and waited next to the spinning door for the car to pull into the hospital lot.

A black Caprice Classic huffed its way into the circular drive and honked its horn like a date from the 1970s, and Blake made sure the wrap on his head was in place before shuffling out into the brazen wind. He yanked at the crooked door handle and finally got it open, sat on slightly cracked vinyl and inhaled gas station cigarettes and too many spritzes of Cool Water. "What's up, baby," the driver said in a high-pitched voice that seemed to cackle with delight and irreverence. "Where you headed?"

"Just over to 1500 Central Avenue, the two-story house on the corner of Martin Drive."

"I got you." They pulled away slowly and made their way toward downtown. "You alright, your shit is bleeding a little, dog. You get in an accident?"

"I'm good," Blake said, and adjusted the wrap on his head a little. "Got jumped earlier, two guys outside the Mill talking shit."

"These white boys are tripping out here, ain't they," the guy said, knowing, somehow, what the deal was with his assailants.

"Don't know what their problem was," Blake offered, and slumped back in his seat, listened to the driver rail against crazy people against the backdrop of booming trap bass. For the first time all night he let the weight of the attack hit him, let the reverberations of the music rattle his chest and his head as he thought about the blatant hostility of the guys, the unnatural vitriol in their voices. He hadn't experienced that, neither he nor Tyner had really been touched by the kind of deep antagonism that the rednecks and white trash of Hudson County seemed to hold so firmly to. Tyner played ball, Blake was his friend and had a doctor for a dad and a white mom. Fairly or not, they'd sailed through life, but as he neared home he could only ask himself how he'd let that happen, how did he let two racist losers tear him down.

The ride came to an end and he peeled off $20 for the driver, told him to keep the change, and opened the door. "Hey, don't let these fools mess with you like that," the guy said as he twisted in his seat and looked back at Blake. "Hold yourself up, brotha, stay strong."

"Thanks, I appreciate it," Blake said, and reached over the top of the seat for an old-school handshake. Inside his apartment, he stripped down and got in the shower, careful to keep his head away from the spray, and doused his body in hot water and a cedar- and lime-scented body wash. He finished, swished around some mouthwash and ran his electric toothbrush across his uppers and lowers and tongue, went to the kitchen for aspirin and cold water, and fell into bed a little before 3 o'clock and disappeared into an uncomfortable, unfamiliar sleep.

As promised, Lena called, waking up Blake as she ended her shift at 7 and walked to the Volkswagen parked next to the security guard's white Ford Escape. "Sorry to call so early but I wanted to make sure your head isn't pounding or feeling dizzy," she breathed into the phone.

"No, it's OK. No signs of a TBI or anything," he said as he rolled over onto his back and stared up at the swirls of stucco on the ceiling. "And I took 600 mg of ibuprofen before I went to sleep."

"Well, that's good to hear. Did Kelly say when you need to go back to get the staples out?"

"Kelly? Oh, the PA, yeah in four or five days, I'll probably go back Wednesday."

"If you're feeling up to it, can we maybe hang out on Thursday, then? A late lunch, if that works, I have to be at the hospital by 6:30."

"Absolutely." He scrolled through the rolodex of restaurants in his head that fit his meager budget and weren't basic fast-food or fast-casual. "I know a place not far from downtown, they make great gyros, falafel, shawarma, hummus, that kind of thing. Sound good?"

"Oh yeah, great. God, it feels like I've been eating nothing but lettuce and yogurt and chicken salad for months. Is 2 o'clock too late for you?"

"No, not at all, I can meet you then."

"Take care of your head, Blake, call me if you need anything or don't want to wait until Wednesday if you have a question about something." He heard, in the background, the closing of a car door and the revving of an engine before her voice returned. "Although it sounds like you know what's up." She said goodbye and he tried to go back to sleep but couldn't get the sound of her raspy voice, slightly tinged with both professionalism and worry, out of his head.

He went to the bathroom to splash cold water on his face and rub his eyes and check the damage, spotted a tiny nick with yellowish tint appeared below his eye, and the cut in his head didn't seem that bad, even with a little bit of swelling at the site. Invigorated, for a moment, he went to the kitchen, gulped down some water as his extra large cup of coffee brewed, then emailed his editors to let them know of his injury and ask for a couple of days off. The coffee felt good, tasted good, and he let the bed lure him back, found a cache of *Fresh Prince of Bel-Air* episodes on a DVD and indulged himself for a few hours. Mariana called him and asked if he could shovel the drive so she could head to the store, and he explained, as simply and undramatically as he could, that he probably shouldn't strain himself with manual labor or the cold weather, and after some minute details his mom was up the door and in his apartment and checking on him.

"You should have called me from the hospital, I would have been there for you," she said starkly.

"Mom, it was late, and I was fine, it's just a little cut, see? A few staples to stop the bleeding, that's the only reason I even went to the ER, if it was earlier I would have gone to urgent care."

"Blake, you always say you're fine, that you don't need me, that everything is OK and everything's going to be OK." She moved closer and sat on the side of the bed, her eyes, faded into the mildest of blues, drilling into him with an intensity he hadn't seen in years. "Your father did the same thing, he never talked about what was happening inside, and when he died, I felt like there was such a huge part of me that never really knew him, and I don't want the same thing to happen to you, I don't want you to bury everything inside and keep people away."

He sniffed and sat up, rubbed his bare arms and looked at the floor, not wanting to return her gaze. "But that's you," he said. "That's how you feel about me. I have to live in my shoes every day, and if I was ever in trouble, deep trouble, I would come to you, for sure."

She pulled back, a little, and her look changed, her warmth gone, and she stood up. "So there's nothing going on, there's nothing wrong with how you're living your life, right?"

"What? Why are you saying it like that? You know what happened, you said it was cool for me to come home and figure things out."

"I did. And it's been three years."

"Am I on a time limit? You need progress reports?"

"Blake, what I said about your dad, that's all true," she started to back away, to the door, but kept her eyes on him. "But he accomplished something, he worked hard, he built a life and a family."

"Mom," he said, his voice almost shaking as she neared the door. "Come on, you're acting like you don't understand."

"Just do whatever you want," she said and pulled the door handle. "By the way, your Aunt Meena called me, Uncle Joe is really sick, she wants you to go see him." Her footsteps echoed down into the garage, and he heard the outside door slam shut, leaving him to wrestle with what did matter, not his dad, not his mom, but the entire nature of who he was and who he'd be.

It had been a while, months or even a year, since he'd been to Louisville, and the drive across the bridge felt odd with the sheen of snow on so many surfaces and the mist atop the Ohio River. Instead of continuing downtown or east, he veered south on the Watterson Expressway, got off and turned into the small neighborhood wedged between Rubbertown and the north end of Shively. He checked the little slip of paper with Meena and Joe's address and pulled in front of a small yellow house with a blue truck buried under the snow in the driveway and a white Buick Regal behind it.

"Just come on in," Meena had told him when he talked to her the day before, but he didn't feel comfortable just pushing inside, knocked on the door, turned the handle and announced himself as he walked into the living room.

"Hey baby," a female voice said from the couch, and he smiled at Meena sitting down, walked over and leaned down for a hug. "How you doing?" The smell of cigarettes hovered over her and immediately attached itself to his fleece and his jeans, and he tried not to cough or scrunch up his face in disgust.

"OK, I guess. Working, you know." He hesitated, couldn't remember if she knew about Tyner's fame or their friendship, it was hard to tell sometimes what news travelled across the river and became well-known to the family. "Sorry I haven't been over in a while. Landa, too, she couldn't come today."

"That's alright, I know ya'll busy," she said, exhaled a large cloud and pointed to the bedroom down the hall. "We ain't going nowhere."

"So Joe's not doing too good, huh?"

"He hasn't been good for a while, but he wanted to talk to you, that's why I called your momma. Go on in."

Blake looked down the hall, saw the obligatory black household pictures hanging on the walls, Martin and Ali and JFK and Barack and Michelle. The bedroom was at the end, past a small bathroom and the entry to the kitchen, and he walked slowly to the doorway and tapped on the frame before going in.

"Uncle Joe?"

"Yeah, who's that, Blake? Come on in here," Joe rasped from under a bulky white sheet, and Blake slid in, his feet nearly catching on an upturned corner of carpet. The regular bed sat empty, Joe's hospital bed had been placed on the other side, near the window, with a little table in between covered in bottles of medication and tissues and remote controls and a tall Styrofoam cup half-filled with green soda and a little white roach motel. Joe shifted and struggled to push himself up with his skinny arms, and Blake stared at the bed, there was little movement coming from the bottom, and he realized both his legs were missing, amputated above the knee.

"Hey, Joe." He had nothing to add, no way of knowing where to take the conversation, their connection had been his dad, Nelson, Joe's younger brother, and without that connection the relationship naturally ebbed and dissolved, and Blake had done nothing to fix it.

"Come here, man, let me get a look at you. Can't see too damn good, plus she got it dark as hell in this room." Blake sidled up next to the bed and was hit with the smell of flesh and urine. Joe reached out, and Blake gently shook his hand. "You look too much like your momma, I barely see your daddy in you. Not like Landa. Not even like Grady."

"Grady?" From the living room a tremulous voice came from a small pair of speakers, Al Green crooning over an organ about the good times, and for a moment Blake flashed to the family dinners and cookouts of his teenage years, after Joe moved in with Meena and her kids, and summer and fall nights became feasts of ribs and burgers and brats and chicken and late-night games of spades on the deck and nothing but R&B and soul music that Blake knew from the first note. He also flashed to the times he'd hated being in the house, when Meena's kids made fun of him for being too light skinned and chased him around the neighborhood, and the time he had to clean himself up in the open shower in the basement. There was no curtain or covering of any kind, and he'd cowered alone in the corner while cold water blasted him from a rusty shower head and swirled at his feet on the concrete floor.

"He was your brother, your older brother, you never knew about him, your sister and your momma didn't, either." A stab of pain seemed to hit Joe in the midsection, and he doubled over as far as he could, leaned to the little table and grabbed the cup and hacked something foul-looking into it. "Your daddy had him a long time ago with a girl from back home, but they were never really together."

"You're saying my dad has another kid? Why didn't he ever say anything?"

"He had his reasons, I suppose, trying to become a doctor, start his business over there, start his family with Mariana, felt it was best to keep quiet on that."

"OK, so why are you telling me? Why now?"

"You do what you feel, I just wanted to say my piece while I still can. My heart, this diabetes, it ain't gonna be long for me," he said with a weird little smile. "People get strange and get to talking at these points, I always thought it was foolish when I'd see all the old folks calling in their kids and grandkids to talk, but that's just how it goes."

"A brother. Whoa," Blake said quietly. "So where is he, Grady? How do I get in touch with him?"

"You can't, like I said he was your brother, but he's gone, been gone."

"Really? What happened?"

"Your daddy killed him."

Chapter 15

The wind rushed at him, and he tugged his gloves tighter to keep out the swirling cold. Beneath him, the engine groaned and growled and spit itself awake and he backed out, began his rounds, his mind barely registering the work or the rough ground underneath him or the relentless chill in the air. He'd done everything he was supposed to, followed the script as tightly as possible, accomplished everything perfectly. But the fury remained, the ache still throbbed within him. There was no way to dispose of it, he saw the faces, the hands, the feet, he smelled the hogroot, he felt the plush give of the snow and the disappearance of his boots. He had to do something, he realized, to relieve the anger. To make the feeling finally go away.

"Hold still, please, don't move." The PA's voice, firm and authoritative, shot into Blake's ear, and he grimaced in response, wondering if the anesthetic for getting the staples removed was going to do anything to alleviate the pain of having small metal prongs pulled out of his skull. It hurt, a little, and he held a piece of gauze to his head after and walked out in good spirits, drove home and emailed his editor to say he'd be up for an assignment the next day.

His phone rang and he saw his mom's face pop up, answered on the second bleep. "Yeah?"

"Blake, you need to come over here," she said bluntly and hung up. He went over in the clothes he'd worn to the hospital, heavy blue sweatpants and a slightly mangy long-sleeve Rose-Hulman shirt, saw a large black sedan parked on the street, walked in through the back door and gently looked around the corner of the living room at the front door. Two men were standing with his mom, one wearing khakis and polos underneath his coat, the other a state trooper in winter gear.

"Hello," Blake said with a slight wheeze. "Can I help you?"

"Hi, Blake, I'm Detective Lawrence with the Troy City police department, and this is Sgt. Reuben with the Indiana State Police. We just had a few questions for you if you don't mind."

"Sure," Blake answered, but quickly remembered the meeting he'd had with Tyner and searched his memory for the lie they'd come up with. "What about?"

"Well, we're just asking around about some things that happened a few weeks ago, trying to figure out some details and everything." Both flipped open their little notepads and held a pen over the paper and looked hard at Blake. "Do you remember what you were doing on the night of the 14th? Would have been a Thursday night."

"Yeah, you mind if I look at my calendar real quick? I'm a visual person," he said, held it up to show the cops the blank squares on his app, then quickly scanned the screen and nodded a little. "The 14th, I had to work, I had an assignment due, an article. Then I hung out with my friend Tyner, we watched a movie at his place, and I left around 10."

"So did you call or text him that day or maybe the day before?"

"Uh, no," Blake stammered a little, thinking about the lie as it expanded and morphed. "I ran into him at a game in December and we planned to meet up, the 14th was the nearest date we could find that worked for both of us."

"What'd you watch?" the state cop asked.

"It was a Marvel movie, the Captain America one where he argues with Iron Man and all the Avengers fight. *Civil War*, I think it's called."

"And you're sure it was the 14th? No mistaking it for another day?"

"Yeah, it was the same day I turned in my story." He clicked on his email app and showed the detective his sent mail, which wasn't much in the way of evidence but seemed to satisfy the guy for the moment.

"And you left around 10, you said?"

"Yes, maybe a little after, but I remember looking at the clock in my car as I was driving home and it was 10:10."

"Have you heard anything recently about Mr. Hayes, noticed him acting out of the ordinary or behaving in a manner you found abnormal?"

"No, same old Tyner, didn't notice anything different with him."

"If you think of anything, if you remember something, give us a call," the detective said, and handed him a business card. "Thanks for your time."

"No problem,' he said, and watched his mom follow the guys to the door and close it behind them.

"So what's that all about? Is Tyner in trouble?" Mariana asked.

"No, mom, he's fine, they're just checking out alibis and stories and crossing their I's and all that."

"You were with him then? That night?"

"Do you remember me being around? Remember my car here?"

"Well, no, it was gone."

"See?" he said, and put his head down as he moved to the kitchen. "Not a big deal."

"Blake," she said loudly, and he stopped in front of the refrigerator and looked back. "Did he have anything to do with it?"

Their eyes locked, and he wondered if she was trying to coerce something out of him, a confession of an unimaginable sin that he had a part in. But he knew the truth, or at least a major part of it. "Mom, no, absolutely not," he said as he headed for the back door. "Don't ever ask me that again." He retreated to his apartment, willing himself to keep the lie held down, although he believed it was being told for the right reasons. Not like his past fabrications and cover stories. The trip to Indianapolis with the girl? He told his mom he had an interview with the assistant dean at a medical school. The drive to Philly, when he missed a final and supplied Tyner with clean urine? He kept that completely under wraps and told his mom he needed to stay in Terre Haute an extra couple of days to help a friend move.

Even the newest lie, the bombshell dropped by Uncle Joe, he knew he had to trap it within himself, not tell his mom or his sister that his father had another kid and seemingly raised him for years. Blake found it implausible that his dad had really killed his own child, the abruptness of the phrase didn't sit right with him and he had to ask further and probe until Joe revealed that it was a crash on the interstate that ended Grady's life, and Nelson was behind the wheel.

The control over his emotions faded, and he slammed his fist into the wall as he stomped around the apartment, trying to conceptualize a story to tell himself about why it should all remain a secret. He was tired of secrets, tired of the respect given to the way his family withheld and evaded and compensated for their misfortunes and misdeeds with endless fiction. Tired of the hellacious joke that consumed him at all times, that no matter what he did, no matter who he cared for, his life was surrounded by a sea of darkness that he could never get out of.

The memory dropped on him from out of the sky: the halo of ash and smoke singeing his nostrils with every breath, a cold breeze slicing through gaps in the concrete structure, the buzz of fluorescent lights overhead, the exhaust of minivans and SUVs chugging in and out of the parking garage in a near constant stream, the unnatural warmth of the November evening and the clammy feel of his skin under the beige cardigan and Henley shirt.. They didn't go to the casino too much, he and Tyner, they weren't that into slots or blackjack or poker, and the large open gaming room made them both feel a little vulnerable, especially since Tyner had only been back in Troy for a year and was still enormously popular. But the boys had come home for Thanksgiving and wanted a big night out, so they filled three cars with friends and girls and went to dinner and then headed west to the casino, which was tucked between the side of a hill and the swarming river, and seemed to jump out of the landscape after miles of open, empty country roads. Jessie came along, she'd been home with Jazmin for months and practically begged to be invited, and she and Tyner drank copious amounts of alcohol, in all manner and variety, more than Blake had seen from either of them, wine with dinner and beers at the machines and syrupy cocktails at the tables and multi-colored shots on the dance floor of the adjoining club.

Something sparked in Jessie, maybe an interested look from a woman toward Tyner, maybe a poorly-timed comment, but the final 30 minutes were spent listening to their arguing and bickering and rehashing of long-buried conversations, all against the backdrop of the pings and bings and bells and dings of the casino floor. Blake urged Tyner and Jessie to head out to the car, offered to drive them back home and then return for the rest of the group, and the three walked out slowly, Jessie cradling the rest of her drink in a small plastic cup and Tyner ignoring her and looking at his phone.

"Shit, I forgot the keys with Les, I'll be right back." Blake sprinted back to the casino, showed his ID to the security guard, jogged back to the club and spotted Les with two girls standing at the end of the bar. He shouted over the din of electro-pop busting from the invisible speakers, grabbed the keys, jogged back through the highway of patterned carpet and bright machines and smoldering gamblers, hopped a set of stairs and ran to the car at the far end of the lot. A little scream, muted and muffled, caught his attention, but he didn't see anyone standing by the doors. Something scraped along the ground, and he went around to the passenger's side and saw Tyner.

"The hell is wrong with you!" Tyner growled through clenched teeth, and Blake didn't move, looked at Jessie on her back, her legs flailing and her arms in front of her face. Tyner was leaning over her, his eyes blazing, his mouth snarling, and as he cocked his right fist, Blake ran over and put his hands on Tyner's shoulders to move him away.

"Chill out, man, cut that shit out," he said loudly, but Tyner pushed him to the side and went back to Jessie.

"Don't fuck with me, Jessie," Tyner shouted, and Blake got back in between them and tried to shield Jessie's body from Tyner's wrath. "Don't fuck around with me. Blake, get this bitch outta here, get her the hell outta here." The scuffle continued, Blake lifted Jessie up, who ran at Tyner and, with all of her strength, took a swing and connected with his jaw.

"Come on, ya'll love each other, right? Stop it," Blake tried to calm them down and failed, and a small group of people walked down the center of the lane, pointed and yelled as Jessie screamed obscenities at Tyner, then a minute later a small white car with a flashing light pulled up and two security officers got out.

"What's going on here?" shouted one of the guards, his mouth almost hidden amidst a massive goatee. "Ma'am, what's happening, are you all right?"

"She's cool, everything's cool," Tyner said as he held his hands up.

"Sir, I'm not talking to you. Ma'am, are these two causing you a problem?"

Jessie stood her ground next to Blake, the RPMs and adrenaline forcing such rapid breathing that her chest couldn't seem to keep up with the pace and she had to force herself to pause and gulp in air. "It's fine, we were just having a disagreement." Her eyes stayed fixated on Tyner, she didn't seem to notice Blake standing in front of her and never looked at the security guards.

"Are you involved in this? What's your story?" the second guard asked Blake, and he looked over and kind of shrugged.

"We came here together, as a group, the rest are inside, they wanted to leave and I had to get the car keys." He lifted the keys to show the guy, looked at Tyner for confirmation that he was responsible for the direction of the lie, and continued. "They were having an argument, a regular couples thing, nothing physical, they were just loud and causing a scene, and I got in between them to calm things down but me and Jessie fell down next to the car."

"Ma'am, is that true? Do we need to call the police?"

"You heard what he said," Tyner growled, and both guards pushed in a foot or two, their hands poised over walkie talkies and night sticks.

"Are you sure you're OK?" they reiterated, ignoring Tyner. "We can have the police here in a few minutes so you can make a formal statement."

"There's no need to call anyone," Blake said, still playing negotiator and peacemaker, his natural inclination to quell conflict and relate to authority figures emerging, and the guards seemed to relax a little. "You remember Tyner Hayes? The basketball player? People still go crazy when they see him, right?

He's like Larry Bird and Pervis Ellison all in one, and some women overreacted to seeing him and Jessie thought Tyner was getting too friendly, but he's super nice to the fans, man. Autographs, pictures, hugs, he does everything."

"Wait, you're Tyner Hayes?" the guard with the goatee asked, and Tyner nodded, leaned forward for a handshake, and the tension lifted instantly. "Wow, I didn't even recognize you, you're so much taller in person."

"Yeah, it's me," Tyner murmured, then stepped toward Jessie and reached his arm out and put it around her waist. "I'm sorry for the commotion, we've had a few drinks, out celebrating, you know, and got a little loud and a little crazy. Sorry about all this."

"It's fine, we get calls like this all the time. As long as you're OK." The guards looked at Jessie, no longer with the desperation of wanting to crush their evening, and she nodded, put her own arm around Tyner's waist, and the guards nodded their approval and went back to their little car and drove away as the small crowd dispersed. Blake looked at Jessie, wondered why she put up with Tyner, why she didn't come to her senses and see what Blake was capable of. Jessie waited in the car while Blake took Tyner inside, grabbed little bottles of water from the bar, and tracked down the rest of the crew and told them all it was time to go.

Whiffs of Arabian folk music greeted them as they walked into Tariq's Grill, along with the intense smells of basmati and pita and rosewater and coriander and gamey grilled meat. Blake pointed to a small yellow table against the wall and followed Lena, who sat down before he had a chance to pull her chair out with a flourish of chivalry. In a matter of seconds, a short teenage girl with dark hair, a black shirt, and a pink scarf approached their table with glasses of water and menus, dropped them and moved away without uttering a word, and Blake took a sip while taking the opportunity to look at Lena while she was preoccupied with looking at the appetizers and drinks and various forms of wrapped food.

Lips too thin, skin too pale, the bangs of her red hair cut a little too sharply, the angles of her body a little too acute. But she exuded a quality Blake hadn't encountered too many times in his life, a combination of wit and confidence and deep intelligence and class and a rare, almost indescribable kind of sexiness, like she wasn't interested in how she was perceived by men, only with how good she felt. And Blake knew he wanted her in a way he had never wanted another woman before.

"So how's your head, are you experiencing any side effects?"

"No, everything's good. PA did a good job, I barely notice where the scar is and it's only been a day."

"You know, the way you've been talking, it almost seems like you have some medical training. Is that true or am I just misreading things?"

"Um, I do have a little," he said, and averted his eyes for a second to take a sip and glance at the menu. "My dad was a doctor, so I know a lot just from growing up around him."

"Oh, he was? Does he still practice?"

"No, he passed away a few years ago."

"Oh. Oh, I guess I should have known that, I'm so sorry."

"No, it's fine. We all have something heavy back there we're dealing with."

"I guess that's true." The girl came back and Blake deferred to Lena, who pointed to the menu and ordered three pieces of falafel, hummus and pitas, and fattoush salad, along with a mint tea, and Blake chose a beef and lamb shawarma with fries and a mango lassi.

"So what made you choose medicine? Was that a lifelong goal or something that came up gradually?" Blake asked as the server left with the menus tucked under her arm.

"My mom worked as an ICU nurse for about 20 years, but she never pushed me to do anything specifically in the medical field. Dad is a manager at an insurance office." The tea came, and she delicately lifted the cup to her mouth and softly blew across the green surface. "I don't know, I just wanted to be someone important and wanted to really help people, whatever that means."

"Can I ask you something else? Something maybe a little weird?"

"I guess so."

He paused to gather his thoughts and looked at Lena's cheeks, which had flushed bright pink in the warmth of the restaurant.

"Were you at the funeral? For Jessie and the kids? I thought I saw you getting into your car after the service."

"Yeah, I did go. Probably not a good idea, I didn't know anyone and it's not really, like, professional to do that. But I couldn't get it out of my mind." She stopped and reached for her water, put it down and grabbed a napkin. "I saw them at the hospital, the mom, the little kids, and I shouldn't have been messed up by it, this is what I'm trained for, right? But it got to me, yeah."

"Did it help at all? Or just make you more confused and angry?"

"Um, probably didn't help, but I felt like I needed to go, for some reason."

"Hey, Hummel," a booming male voice resonated in the small restaurant, and they turned to see a guy with thinning brown hair and glasses walking toward them. "How are you doing?"

"Dr. Lowery, hi. Just having lunch," Lena said, and nodded to Blake.

"Blake, what's up," the guy said and reached out for a convoluted handshake that Blake did his best to go through with while keeping a straight face.

"Hey, doc," he said simply.

"You can't resist the gyros either, can you Hummel? I come here once a week."

"This is my first time, actually, Blake recommended it."

"Good call, Blake, I wish you were still at the hospital, you were always fun to have around." He moved to the counter and paid for two massive bags of food, then grabbed the handles and headed for the door. "Hey, Hummel, you working tonight?"

"Yep, seven to seven."

"Ok, well I might still be there, take it easy," he said as he headed out into the winter chill and buffeted his face against the icy wind by lifting the collar on his black topcoat.

Blake looked at her and slowly sipped the fruity smoothie. "Hummel? What's that mean?"

"It's some silly nickname a lot of the docs at the Hud gave me when I first started there."

"So Hummel, like the figurines?"

"Yeah, I'm surprised you even know what they are, it's kind of a Northern European thing, like everyone from Wisconsin and Minnesota have them."

"My mom has a couple of them in the house. She's from Germany."

"Oh. Oh, ok, I see," Lena said, and eyed Blake more intensely than she had since they arrived.

"Not a very good nickname, if you ask me."

"What do you mean?"

"Come on. Delicate, childlike, porcelain little statues? That doesn't fit you at all."

"Well, thanks. Do you have a nickname, something your friends called you growing up?"

"Not really. Sometimes they'd call me B, or Prince, cause of my last name." The food arrived and they paused for a couple of minutes to get the initial tastes out of the way and rave about how great everything was. Lena offered him a bite of all her food, and he sheared a few pieces of meat out of the pita and stabbed some of the seasoned fries on his fork for her. "Before we leave, we have to make sure we order some baklava. Unless you have a condition that prevents you from being drowned in honey and nuts."

"Sure, sounds delicious." She finished off her salad and wiped her mouth, then crossed her legs and gave him another intense look. "Do you bring a lot of people here? A lot of dates, I should say."

"Dates? No, I usually come on my own for lunch, or take some home for me and mom for dinner. I'm not seeing anyone right now."

"Blake, come on, it's OK. I'm a grown woman, I asked around about you. And I'm not blind." She picked up her cup, black on the outside and white on the interior, and drained the rest of the tea. "I know what women are probably like around you, and that's fine. I just don't want to pretend you're something you're not, and I'd like you to be honest with me about who you are."

"I don't know who you talked to," he began, then thought better of it. He could tell she wasn't interested in platitudes or justifications for his past actions. Just a window into who he was and how he looked at himself. And a way to feel comfortable with where she wanted to take things. "It doesn't matter, I guess. I'm not a player or a user if that's what you're thinking. Yeah, I've been with a decent number of women here in Troy, and a few in college. It's a small town, people talk, I get it. But since I left medical school, I've mostly been on my own. Haven't had a real relationship in years. A couple of flings, one that just ended. But until I met you, no one with any potential for something meaningful. Something real."

"OK. So why me, why now?" she said softly.

"Why? I mean, I could give you a list, I've compiled one already," he said, and she laughed and ducked her head awkwardly. "But I don't need any reasons, I know what I see and I know what I've found and I know what I believe."

"What do you believe?"

He returned the look, with the same level of intensity. "That life is precious, and rare, and if you get lucky, a little bit of happiness gets thrown at you.

"And when it does, it's best to just trust it."

Chapter 16

They didn't talk much. They kept things simple. Blake drove his car, followed Lena to her shotgun house on Governor Street, kicked his way through the unshoveled snow on the sidewalk to her front door and she let him in after parking in her little garage out back. He slipped out of his Penguins and jacket and trailed her into her room. She stood motionless by the bed, beckoning him silently, and he walked over, his heart revving up but not yet pounding.

They smiled, that's what he remembered the most. Laughter kicked around the room, contented sighs, and when they looked at each other in the semi-darkness of the room, big stupid grins broke out. He lay on his back and breathed in the scents of her and the small house she occupied, trying to analyze his body and his emotions and come up with the appropriate word in his mind to describe what they'd just done. And settled on something he didn't realize he'd missed in all the times he'd been with a woman: fun.

"Are you doing anything else today?" Lena asked him as she slipped from under the sheet and walked to the bathroom, not bothering to cover up or shield her body, and he smiled at her harmonious audacity.

"Not that I know of. My editor hasn't emailed me a new assignment yet even though I told her my head is fine." He thought for a second about his blog, then said, "I might do a little writing, anyway."

"Ok," she said at the same time as the toilet flushed and came back, still naked, and dropped into bed again. "Do you have any other jobs or do you just write for one place?"

"No, just the one right now."

"You know, when Dr. Lowery saw you, he said he missed you at the hospital. Did you work there or something?"

"No, I never worked there. My dad suggested I volunteer there in high school so I could put it on my college applications, and I worked briefly as a tech in the emergency department one summer, so I know a lot of the staff."

"Why did he want you to do that? I assume he wanted you to go to med school, as well."

"Yeah," he paused, and inserted a slightly panicky cough. "I did, actually, for a little while. But I dropped out."

"You went to med school? Where?"

"Ohio State. For a semester and a half, basically."

"And you dropped out, why? I mean, sorry, I don't mean to bug you." Lena shifted under the blanket and Blake tried not to peak underneath. "So, what happened?"

"I don't think anything happened, really. The curriculum wasn't a problem, grades were fine after the first semester. I came home that Christmas break, and it wasn't long after that my dad died. And I felt like I was only there, at Ohio State, trying to be a doctor, for him," he said. "Plus, I don't know, I felt like I wanted to go out and live my life instead of studying and working nonstop just for the money and prestige."

"That's what you think being a doctor's about?" she said with the faintest whisper of annoyance.

"No, that's what it felt like I was doing it for. And I realized I didn't want to work that hard or study that hard or devote myself to something so altruistic when I knew I didn't have that in me anymore."

"Because of your dad," she said quietly, and he nodded back at her. Maybe it was the truth, maybe it was his father's death that had fucked him up. But he didn't have the sense of honesty to tell her what really went down. Not yet.

They talked for another 20 minutes, longer than he'd ever spent with a woman in bed without pursuing or being pursued or indulging in his refractory period. She told him, reluctantly, that she needed an hour of sleep before work, and he kissed her on the cheek, the forehead, and the lips before putting on his clothes and saying goodbye.

He'd wake up early, too early, four or five in the morning, and reach for the alarm clock that wasn't beeping at him. He'd sit through classes without uttering a word. He'd watch shows on his laptop alone while his roommates ate pizza and poured over notes in the dining room. He'd ignore the sumptuous stares of comely undergrads and dismiss the aggressive approaches from soon-to-be professional women. He'd spend hours researching the effects of ADHD medication and birth rates. He'd sleep two or three hours. He'd do it all the next day.

His mother noticed a change when he came home, a lethargy and lack of energy in even the most basic of tasks, but chalked it all up to the pressures of his first semester at Ohio State. He'll get better, she thought, once he gets through the initial, grueling course load and finds his true calling. So she kept her distance, ignored his lack of appetite, his sullen appearance, his bummy outfits, and wished him well when he took off for school on Jan. 2.

He didn't remember how he got there. He'd never been there. He couldn't recall ever seeing the place before. But he was there, somehow, in some kind of ancient rec center. Whatever state he'd been in came to an abrupt end, and he found himself sitting on a rickety metal folding chair, the only lights coming from a glowing green exit sign and a fluorescent bulb radiating out of an adjacent kitchen. After a few minutes of getting his head reoriented, he searched his pockets, found nothing, no wallet and no phone and no keys, and got up in search of a door.

"Can I help you?" a friendly voice echoed from a doorway, and Blake tried to focus through the dimness.

"Where am I?"

"Excuse me? How'd you get in here?"

"I don't know, something happened and I woke up here?"

"Son, you're in St. Mark's Church, in the cafeteria. Did you come in through the front?" The man started to approach but stopped and flipped on the overhead lights. "Are you on anything, do I need to call for help?"

"No, I haven't taken drugs. I'm a med student."

"OK." The man came closer and Blake squinted into a gray beard and glasses and shaggy brown hair. "I'm Patrick Vinegar, I'm the associate pastor. Do you have a friend or roommate I can call for you?"

"I can't, I don't have my phone, I don't have anybody's number."

"What about your car?"

"I don't have anything." He felt wobbly but held the pastor's gaze. "Are you gonna arrest me? Is this a trap or something?"

"No. Son, are you having a problem?"

"You got me in here, now you're trying to keep me for some reason." Blake shook his head, trying to loosen the tangle of confusion inside, then picked up the folding chair and flung it across the room and hustled away from the pastor as it crashed into the concrete wall, pushed his way against a set of metal double-doors and into the gun-metal evening.

A small side street ran next to the building and out to the main road, which he struggled to recognize in the waning light of the day and with no visible landmarks in sight. He looked around, the street appeared empty, as did the adjoining parking lot, but finally spotted his Camry haphazardly wedged between a pair of black dumpsters behind the church. With some effort he yanked open the door, the icy temperature nearly freezing it shut, and inside the keys dangled from the ignition, and his wallet and phone had fallen in the gap between the seat and the middle console. For a moment, as he settled his sunken, gaunt frame into the cold seat and turned the car on and waited for the engine to warm up, he sat without moving, stared out the front window into the dull brick. Then he dropped his head, and his eyes welled with tears, and he wept.

A knock on the window nearly shattered him, and he jerked his head around to see the face of the pastor. "Young man, I think you should come back in," the muffled voice said. "You seem like you could use some help." Blake didn't respond, shoved the gear shift into reverse and backed into the street and tore off toward his off-campus apartment. Two days later, he left Columbus for good.

The afterglow. Better than he'd ever experienced before. The talking. The comfort. Everything felt good and right and worthy of remembrance, and as he headed back to his apartment he debated calling her and leaving a message, just to hear her the sweetness of her voice and to tell her how much he'd enjoyed their time together.

But he declined, even he knew that would be pushing it a little, and he went inside and tried to keep from smiling too much as he opened his laptop and ignited his mix of Al Green, Teddy P, Luther, Marvin, Bobby Caldwell, Anita Baker, Sade, all the greatest love songs and slow jams and bedroom tunes he'd grown up with and worshipped as the epitome of romance and sex in R&B and soul. He'd always wondered what it would be like to listen to those songs, to hear every note, every word, every whisper and scream, and feel like he understood it all.

The triumphant scream near the conclusion of "I Want You" was on its way, and he prepared to join in and get lifted from his seat, and he felt compelled to open his computer, get to his blog and start writing. He labeled the post "A Deep Attachment," and let his fingers work while his mind flitted through image after image. "She talks and moves like she knows who she is. She thrives under pressure. She is devoted, committed, she doesn't give in to sullenness, she believes and she shows it every time I see her. L Boogie, that's what I'll call her, is a physical force, she is totally in her element no matter where she is, but with me she erupts, crisscrosses and intertwines her body with mine and creates a true excitement that I've never known. The terror and tragedy are still there, but L has occupied me fully. I am excited to find out what every single moment brings."

No hesitation, he hit publish and sat back with a satisfied grin. But a notification on the screen jarred him out of the moment and the cycle of love songs and he clicked on an email from Amos with "t screen" in the subject line. "They haven't officially released but I got word that no drugs were found in Jessie's system. No food either. Just some weird herbs and flowers and roots like marsh clover, gentiana, wormwood, ginger, and a trace amount of alcohol. Thinking she drank something that night but didn't find any in her place, so they're still confused. A."

He clicked around and shut off the music, the quiet of his apartment suddenly stifling, as he roamed through his memories and thought about his interactions with Jessie. Yeah, she'd gotten drunk a few times, but he could never remember her drinking anything that would have resulted in those ingredients lingering in her body. But he stopped himself, he didn't know her anymore, he didn't know her life, and though he doubted she'd be inebriated while taking care of her kids all on her own, he didn't know for sure.

Then something hit him. Tyner, his house, the last time Blake had been over there, a while ago, over a year, Jessie pregnant with Georgy, Tyner in good spirits and celebrating the fact that he was finally going to have a little boy. He showed Blake the custom cigars he'd ordered with "It's a Boy!" stenciled on the cellophane wrapper, the tiny Temple Owls basketball and onesie he wanted to use for the first photo session, even the outfits he wanted to wear in the pictures, a white Calvin Klein tee with a suede jacket and gray slacks for one set, and a black adidas tracksuit for the other. They went to the kitchen and Tyner pulled a gold-labeled bottle of champagne out of the fridge, poured glasses for himself and Blake and offered a sip to Jessie. And on the counter, by the key rack, was a row of liquor bottles, including a tall, prominent green bottle of Jägermeister.

Chapter 17

"No, you have to forget about the proof and the percentages and the packaging and all that. That shit doesn't matter. It's the mash bill, man, it's all about the mash."

"I know, but it's just numbers, man, water and corn and wheat and whatever mixed together, the barrels and the aging and the percentage are more important."

"I never even seen you drinking bourbon, you probably think red wheat is the king when it comes to whiskey."

"You think cause I don't drink that shit around you I don't know what I'm talking about?" Chris slammed his bottle of Miller Lite on the counter and stumbled back off his stool. Casey looked in their direction but stayed quiet, and Blake drank the rest of his Rittenhouse while keeping his eyes forward. Not their first drunken argument, and Casey knew not to get involved too early, they'd typically raise their voices over something stupid for a few minutes and then quiet down, have a few more drinks, and leave an extra $20 or so in tips.

"Hey, you ever drink Jäeger, like for real drink it, not just have a shot?"

"Nah, man, that shit's nasty. It's for college kids and Panama City Beach parties."

"You know anybody that drinks it? Like, they keep a bottle of it around or anything?"

"No, why? Are you looking for a freak who likes bloody, syrupy licorice booze?"

"Just curious, man, damn." Blake pulled out his wallet and left some cash on the counter for Casey, walked out with saying anything more, kept his eyes peeled for the guys who'd roughed him up the previous week, but he hadn't seen anyone like them in Schwarz's since he got there. He pulled his phone out, tried to tap out a message in the cold but gave up, his hands unable to master the tiny digital buttons, and he walked as fast as he could to his car on the street and started the engine but stayed put while he typed.

"I got some news about Jessie. You up?" Didn't wait for a response, pulled out into the street and felt the car slide a little on the slick road, and kept the speed at 25 mph as he tracked through side streets on the way to Tyner's. He wasn't drunk, he figured, but he'd had enough to cause himself a problem if the blue-and-white showed up in his rearview mirror.

The adrenaline ramped up as he neared the neighborhood, the road inclined a few degrees and the Camry struggled a little to make it up to the house, so he parked on the road a couple of houses down, walked through the yard and looked in at the living room through an open window. No movement, but the blazing lights and TV let him know Tyner was awake, so he knocked on the door and stood back a few steps.

"Blake? Yo," Tyner said as he pushed the screen door open and filled the frame. "Whassup?"

"I texted you a little bit ago. You get it?"

"Nah."

"Can I come in? I found out some things about Jessie. About the autopsy."

"All right." Tyner moved aside and Blake walked in, didn't try to hide that he was looking around at everything in the room. The kid's toys remained in the corner, spilled out of a large wooden basket and onto the floor next to stacks of books about fairies and princesses and animals, paintings and drawings flapped on a shelf, little pink shoes had been dropped by the door next to their grown-up counterparts, and Blake remembered the lack of shoes at the crime scene and wondered what had happened to them.

"So no one has called you or talked to, your lawyer or anyone else?" Blake asked as he moved to the couch and sat down.

"Ain't heard a thing," Tyner said and swayed a little as he tried to find the arm of his big recliner and fell into it. Blake recognized the wonky, slow movements, the heavy eyes, and smelled the cheap blended whiskey.

"They didn't find any drugs in her system, just a little bit of alcohol, and some kind of herbs and roots and weird flowers, but they didn't find any bottles or evidence at the little place she was staying with the kids."

"Figured they wouldn't, she didn't keep no drinks around."

"Did she get it here or something?"

"Nah, man, I ain't seen her in weeks, just the kids a couple times."

"Oh." Blake leaned back and looked around some more, there were photographs of the kids still hanging, the formal pictures of Tyner and Georgy, but no indication that Jessie had ever lived there. No photos, no feminine touches, not even the frilly little pillows that used to adorn the couch. "So you don't know why she really went out that night or what she was up to."

"Why you asking me this shit, I told you and I told everyone, I ain't had nothing to do with what she was up to. She probably got involved with all them crazy mother fuckers from up in Bochim, man."

"So why'd you have me lie to the damn cops if you had nothing to do with anything? Tell me what the hell's going on, I'm not trying to get in trouble over this."

Tyner reached next to his chair and lifted up a rocks glass half-filled with watery brown liquid and took a drink. "Like I said, I can't be having the cops looking at me sideways and thinking I had something to do with this fucked-up situation."

"But why lie? I would have told them you didn't hurt your kids, I know you loved them, you're not a fucking psycho."

"Doesn't matter," he mumbled, and got up from the chair, "doesn't matter, man, they're gone, they ain't gonna find nothing, it's over."

"Who were you with, Tyner?" Blake said and got up, stared at Tyner's back. God, he doesn't care about me, Blake thought, and probably never has. He's not interested in helping people, in helping me, because he's never had to worry about anyone but himself. He's Tyner Hayes, and that's all that matters. "Look, do what you want, but I'm not getting involved with you anymore, not like this. If a cop or anyone comes to me, I ain't lying for you again."

Tyner spun around and seemed to trip a little, but got himself straight, then came at Blake with his hand out, grabbed at Blake's shirt at the collar, and pushed him against the wall. "My best friend," he slurred, and his grip tightened. Blake knew he couldn't handle Tyner physically, even drunk, Tyner had kept himself in shape after basketball, in fact he seemed to be even stronger, and Blake was giving up five inches, about 50 pounds, and the kind of immeasurable drunken power he knew not to mess with.

"Get your hands off me, man. I'm not the one you should be going after," Blake said, as stoic and stern as possible, and Tyner stepped back a bit and loosened his grip. "I came here cause I'm on your side, not because I wanna fight you about some bullshit. You haven't been straight with me, shit, since we were kids. Just talk to me, T."

"Goddamn Blake, you always be on some truth-telling and honesty shit," Tyner said, and backed away, fell into his chair with a grunt. "I don't know what the hell you do all day, who you go see, now you wanna know about me? Alright, fine. Yeah, I was in Louisville, yeah, I got a friend over there I've been seeing, and I ain't told nobody about it. Cause people over here would talk about me and destroy me."

"Come on, it ain't like that anymore."

"Yeah, it is. You ever listened to my mom? You ever listened to the Troy City fans? You know what they'd all do if they find out this shit, and my family's dead, too? I'd be done, man, done." He put his face in his hands, and Blake could hear the kind of sloppy crying he always associated with drunks. But Tyner had never shown that kind of emotion, that kind of vulnerability or weakness, and Blake knew that it was up to him to do his best to help.

"Alright, man, alright. Take it easy, you can figure something out, we can figure it out."

"Yeah, Blake'll take care of it, Blake will handle my shit." Tyner looked up, his eyes weren't dry but he was not sobbing like Blake expected. There was a distance, a coldness, that he didn't recognize, something distinct from the jovial guy he'd always known.

"You just gotta tell the truth, T. Tell the cops where you've been going, get them off your back. It'll go a long way, I promise."

Tyner stood up as Blake moved to the door, and he wrapped his arms around Blake and squeezed, lifted him off the ground a few inches. "You always know the way, man. Always got an answer, always got a solution, I love it." They disengaged after a moment and Blake grabbed the door handle to leave, then turned back to Tyner, who'd fallen back into the chair.

"Hey, I was wondering if you knew anything about Jessie's jewelry. What she wore on a regular basis. Like, I know she had that necklace you bought her, but did she wear anything else?"

"You think I know about everything that girl wore?"

"Well, did she ever wear a cross?"

Tyner stared for a few seconds, then shook his head. "Never seen one before."

Chapter 18

"The information uncovered during the investigation, which was handled thoroughly by the combined efforts of the Hudson County Sherriff's Office and the Indiana State Police, along with assistance from local F.B.I officials, led us to conclude that Jessie Schuetter and her three children, Jazmin, Jett, and Georgy, died from complications due to hypothermia and exposure. Although there weren't any clear or obvious injuries to Miss Schuetter or the children, the Hudson County Coroner's Office conducted autopsies on all the victims to determine a cause of death.

"Right now, we are still searching for answers about why the family was on the St. Aureus campus and whether their deaths were accidental or they were placed there. But, I can assure the families and the community, that we will find the answers to this mystery, I will not rush through anything or skip any steps, no matter how long it takes."

Blake lowered the volume on the TV and let the upheaval settle in his head as he watched the medical investigator, Dr. Dawn Gehlhausen, conduct the press conference with a small cadre of journalists. He spotted the crime reporter, Anne Marie Gill, in the crowd, as well as two of the Louisville correspondents who'd followed things pretty closely. Maybe they knew about the cross, about the girls in Louisville, about the missing shoes, but there was a lot left out from what the public or even the reporters were aware of. And Blake determined, as the coroner finished up and walked away from the lobby of the hospital, that the shock of everything had worn off and he needed to figure out what the hell had happened.

It hit him, then, that he should write some more, but instead of alluding to what was on his mind, dancing around what he knew, he decided to hit the issue with everything he had. "No one is talking about the dead girls in Louisville, about the connection between the crosses found on them and the one found on Jessie, the one she never wore in her life" he typed out. "Someone out there worships the cross, and worships death, and wants to destroy something here that we need to understand." He finished, ran the spell check, and hit publish.

The contents of the newspapers were on the card table he'd pulled up from the garage, two months' of issues of the *Herald-Bulletin*, as well as stories from the *Courier-Journal* he'd printed, which were stacked in a small, neat pile off to the side. It had been a long time since he'd buried himself in work, or given himself over to a cause of some kind. School was school and work was work, but as he started rereading articles, and tracing Jessie's path in her last days, and trying to figure out why everything turned out the way it did, he felt a tinge of exhilaration coursing through his insides, the kind of excitement he used to feel about life, about the challenge in front of him.

A couple of pings from his phone dragged him from the table, and he saw a missed call from Lena and a text from his mom. Later, he thought, and went back to the table, then cracked open his laptop and started searching. Anything, any name, any place. Jessie. Tyner. Troy City. Hudson County. He scanned newspapers from Indianapolis and Nashville and Cincinnati. He looked at small magazines and blogs. The mass of papers and information started to overwhelm him and he plopped back onto his couch, ready to concede that there was nothing out there for him to discover, no key piece of evidence that he could uncover. Pulled up some music on his computer, his dad listened to a lot of the Doobie Brothers and had turned both the kids onto similar 70s rock, and Blake liked the Tommy Johnston era but absolutely loved Michael McDonald and the late 70s albums, put on a rare album cut written and sung by Tiran Porter and tried to keep time with the odd-metered beat and chimed in at the end of the chorus, "Come with me and surely we'll be free."

Something clicked in his head when the playlist kicked over to a new song, a remnant from high school, when only hip-hop dared enter his vernacular and his headspace and tracks from Snoop and Dre still dominated for guys like him. Chronic, he thought, Chronicles, Chroniclers. And he typed in Bochim.

Not the first hit, not the second. Not even the first page drew his eye, he had to click to the second results page to find a result that drew his attention. An article from something called *Indiana Review* with a publication date of March 1999, the premise focused on the intentional community of Bochim in southern Indiana and the charismatic, mercurial, and mysterious leader known as Bezalel. The writer, a woman named Sarah Myers, highlighted many of the key points that Blake and so many people in Troy City knew, the rise of Potters Hill, the emergence of a new leader and the name change, the extreme security and secrecy that surrounded the community, the pragmatic approach to building and sustaining a society within the conservative region of southern Indiana that had never been shy about its distaste for the pious weirdos ensconced in the hills of Hudson County.

The pictures in the article were difficult to see clearly, especially any that featured Bezalel. In the most vivid photo, he appeared tall and thin and shrouded in a long, scraggly beard that obscured his face, but he wore tall brown wading boots that covered his knees, baggy jeans, a long blue suede coat, and a beige hat with dark feathers sticking out of the sides. Two lanky teens stood at his side, and the caption identified them as his sons, Issachar and Manasseh, and a wide-hipped woman in a bulky black top, May, watched over them and clutched a chubby toddler to her chest. Off to the side, near a bush, a little boy, who looked about 11 or 12 years old, held a long piece of rope that stretched into the center of the picture and wound around Bezalel's legs and out of frame.

"My sons will keep this land going after I disappear into the Lord's embrace," the writer quoted Bezalel. "This unconscious way of living has drawn many true believers, who believe with their souls in what we are doing. And though my children have the blood of the Chroniclers in them, I have the utmost faith in the spirit and purity of many of the young ones here, who can allow Bochim to evolve into a place that will touch even the most cynical of hearts. Especially this special young man." The young one, the future of Bochim, according to Bezalel, was the boy in the picture with the rope. Eric.

There were a few more pictures, casual shots of kids swimming, women cooking, men working the fields. It all seemed kooky and harmless, but Blake remembered the dead body from back in the day, he remembered the weird vibe Tyner described on his sole visit, the monstrous freak that accosted Blake just a couple of weeks earlier on the outskirts of the community. There were no other new stories he could find online about Bochim, nothing from the past 10 years or so, and he figured there'd been a brief gap where the leadership decided a bit of local news coverage would help with recruitment or public relations or damage control, and he started a new search to find the writer, Sarah Myers. Maybe, he thought, there's more to that place than she was allowed to reveal.

Too many Sarah Myers' at first, but he narrowed it down to a freelance writer who also worked as an adjunct professor at Eastern Illinois University, just a little more than 50 miles from Terre Haute and the Indiana border. A phone call out of the blue seemed too much, so he sent her an email and explained how he'd come across her article while looking into the Bochim community and the circumstances surrounding Jessie's death. "I don't really know anything right now," he wrote, "but I just have this feeling that there's a connection between someone from up there and what happened to that family."

Less than two hours later, he was half-heartedly working on a small assignment for work, one that would pay him only half of his usual fee, but he needed the $125, badly, especially after he got the bill from his hospital visit. She wrote him back, thanked him for his interest in her old article, then gave her office number and a couple of time slots that she'd be available to speak. "I've got a lot of stories about that place, so get ready."

The next morning, after just one ring, Sarah Myers answered her phone and nearly pierced Blake's eardrum with a high-pitched squeal of a greeting. "I can't believe I'm talking to someone from Troy after all these years," she started. "I swear I haven't thought about that place in so long."

"So you spent a lot of time there when you worked on that article?"

"Not a ton of time, I mostly stayed at a little hotel typing up my notes on a clunky laptop after I interviewed the Bochim people during the day. I maybe went out one time to get a drink, but I was only there for three days and ate gas station sandwiches and hot dogs the whole time."

"I saw a few other stories about Bochim online, but yours seemed to highlight the main guy, the leader, Beza-whatever, the most. What was your take on him as a man, as the guy in charge?"

"Well, I did spend most of my time following him, and he didn't say a whole lot to me, but I think where a lot of reporters would get bored and go off to find someone else to talk to, I stayed and listened, and he wouldn't necessarily talk to me, but he would give orders to people, his second-in-command, Daniel, his wife, and his sons. They weren't very old then, late teens I'd guess, but he put a lot of trust in them."

"Was there anyone else he talked about or talked to?"

"Yes, he really had a tight connection with this kid who was a little bit younger than his sons, a boy named Eric. They'd sit together and whisper and flip through the Bible all by themselves. And then Eric would run off and give orders to all the kids, and some of the boys would just laugh at him and push him away. It was really weird to see, like an odd social experiment gone wrong, you know?"

"Who were Eric's parents, were they high up in the Bochim hierarchy or whatever?"

"Honestly, I have no memory of him being around any adult other than Bezalel. He looked like a little boy but carried himself like a smaller version of the leader, very assured in doling out orders but really awkward around people. I wish I'd written more about the kid but I was trying to capture the whole place, you know? But he was definitely the weirdest one there, even amongst all the other strange people I saw."

"Like who?"

"Oh, gosh, there was an animal wrangler guy who wore baggy jeans and a plaid shirt with the arms cut out and an old *He-Man* hat. And the really big woman that ran the cafeteria who wore a blue Mumu tied with rope around her waist and cooked all day long and never seemed to leave the kitchen. One guy, they called him the architect, he carried a long stick all the time, a staff I guess, and constantly felt the ground, the dirt, scooped up little morsels of it and smelled it and even ate it. And I saw a really, really tall, really skinny man off in the distance, he never came near me, but he almost looked like an albino from afar, with a massive square head and skeletal arms.

"The women seemed to stay away from me, and the matriarch, May, didn't say hello to me at all, the little girls ran and hid in the classroom when I walked near. Almost everyone I talked to was a man, I'm surprised they even let me in the place. Looking back, I'm glad I went with my photographer, David."

"Was there any sense of danger? I mean, did you know about the body found there in the 80s, did they say anything about what happened?"

"I wouldn't say it felt dangerous, just odd. I'd written a lot of stories before that, I have a master's degree in journalism, worked at a few papers, that was the first magazine article that I sold but I had a lot of experience. And that was the first time I really got the sense that I'd better keep them all on my good side, keep them happy. I don't know why, no one threatened me or said anything, it was just a feeling.

"No one ever mentioned the body, I suspected they would have ended the interviews and asked me to leave if I brought it up."

"Ever follow up with them, you or the photographer? As part of your academic work or just out of curiosity?"

"I tried once, about five years ago. There was a number I had for one of the homes, I called and told them who I was and asked to speak to Bezalel, but the woman wouldn't say anything about where he was. Another person got on the line, a man, and told me not to call again. And when I asked if Bezalel was still alive, he hung up. No one answered when I called back, and eventually I just gave up."

"Do you think he's still alive?"

"He might be, I really don't know, if he is he's probably nearly 100 years old."

"One last thing." Blake cleared his throat and looked at the clippings on the table, at one of the pictures of the creek where the bodies were found, at a sheet of paper with the names of the dead girls from Louisville. "What do they really believe up there? What's their ultimate goal for their little community?"

"Well, the leader talked quite a lot about plans for the future of Bochim, about the united interests of the people. He also believed in the synthesis of survival, as he called it, because the old ways of the world would soon collapse and places like Bochim would be models of how to live. He called it empirism, where the leader is not just in charge of his own community but also doesn't recognize anything or anyone as superior to himself, not another emperor, as he called them, not another religion or government, and he keeps everyone safe and living in harmony within their surroundings. It's all a bunch of crap, obviously, but he talked about it with complete sincerity, he truly believed it would come true one day.

"And he believed Eric would be the one to rule over it all."

Chapter 19

She frightened him. She was too smart, too educated, too liberal and unconventional. She didn't answer to anyone, and she was getting too close. He sat and watched her for a long time, she moved a lot, from room to room, rarely sitting down or staying still for long. He liked that about her, at least. And the way she appeared so comfortable with her body and possessed a natural affinity for her imperfections; he liked that, too. But she was a problem, he'd been told over and over, and he had to get rid of her.

It was war, and that meant a way out. His uncles had done it, taken carts and wagons and gone to train stations far away, shipped off to Army bases deep in Louisiana and Texas, and even all the way up in Kentucky. They fought with the 761st Battalion, and the 92nd Infantry, and the 333rd during the Wereth Massacre. All survived, somehow, and returned home to tell of their exploits and adventures across Europe, and all the little boys of Winston County grew up dreaming of being in the Army, the Marines, the Navy. Cumberland Prince, Nelson's father and Blake's grandfather, was assigned to Texas and then to Camp Edwards in South Korea as part of a service support battalion in 1954, and though he never saw direct combat, he received a commendation from the Army and returned home brimming with enough life experience, and enough money, to leave Mississippi and move North. He did so to reunite with some of his relatives, who'd gotten various jobs that allowed for the kind of middle-class life the Prince's had never imagined back in Winston. Though Cumberland wasn't thrilled with Nelson's decision to join the military, the fact that he had a plan to pay for college and then medical school, all during a time when there were no active skirmishes around the world that would potentially threaten his life, made Cumberland OK with everything.

"And now, I'm here," Blake said quietly into the phone. Damn, I've been talking nonstop, he realized, and took a hearty gulp of air and sip from his water bottle. He and Lena agreed to speak on the phone, a rarity for him, but she preferred a real conversation to texting, and with the amount of time she spent at the hospital, and her need for sleep, an in-person visit wasn't feasible, but Blake didn't push, he respected the doctor life. She'd asked about his family, and he gave her more than he'd let on any other time, more than he'd told any woman. Not because it was a sore spot, he was proud of his family and what they'd done, but no one had ever asked, or cared.

"Wow, that's a, wow, what a family history. I wish we'd talked the way your family did about how we ended up where we did."

"Yeah, there was nothing hidden, we didn't keep secrets," he said, his voice catching a little. It wasn't true, he knew, not anymore, but it didn't feel right to call out anyone, not his uncle, not his dad, even though he trusted Lena. "Have you had any visitors from Wisconsin down here?"

"Not yet, I went home for two days in December, I stayed with my parents and had some business to take care of, but no one's come here."

"Hopefully soon," he muttered, and got up to go in the kitchen and look for something to drink, leaned against the counter and opened the refrigerator, hoping for an urge for water or juice, but he gave in and grabbed a green bottle of Dos Equis, uncapped the beer and took a swig. He felt alone, even with Lena talking to him, and the beer wasn't enough to disturb the lock-and-chain aura surrounding him. He dumped the beer in the sink and went back to the couch.

"Lena," he blurted out, and she stopped speaking, waited for what he had to say. "We've been, you know, spending time together, and it's been pretty great. Well, no, it's been amazing, and I just wanted to tell you that I've been thinking a lot recently, about what I've been doing here in Troy, and what I want to happen, you know, from here on out.

"And I feel like it's time to change the sheets, you know, move on, and I don't want you to think this is coming out of the blue. I'm not looking to disappear, but wherever your career takes you, your life, don't be afraid to think of me."

She didn't say a word, Blake couldn't even hear breathing on the line, so he kept going. "I'm not asking you for a commitment, I don't even know that I am asking you for anything specifically. I can have my life, you can have yours, but just keep me in mind, because you've been about the only thing on mine."

"Blake, I don't even know what to say. I mean, that's a hell of a sentiment."

"It is, I know," he said, though he didn't tell her anything more about his desire for change, his sudden desperation to leave Troy and start anew, somehow, to place oceans, endless lengths of highway, between him and the cursed town.

"I can't promise you a thing, I don't know where I'll go, where I'll end up. And I can't give too much of myself to anyone, especially a man, even if it's someone special like you. But you're right, I think we can have our own identities, our own lives, with a person we care about. It's just a matter of determining whether we really are those people. For each other."

They spoke for a while longer, 10 or 15 minutes, and agreed to meet soon, preferably, in Blake's view, at her place. When the call ended, he sat on his couch, his legs splayed off the edges, his hand rubbing his scalp as he wondered why he'd unloaded so much to her, why he'd forgone the ferocious attributes that had held sway over him for so many years in favor of deflecting the pain and dealing with his life as best as he could. Do I already love her, he thought, then shook his head and got up to hunt for his vape pen and make a sandwich. Thought about a movie, a run of TV shows, a slew of records to catalogue his thoughts, but he didn't want anything else in his head, not then.

By the end of the afternoon he was up, packed in a hoodie, and outside, grabbed the mail that his mom always left for him in a metal bin by the back door of her house, since he had his own apartment but not an address. An alumni magazine, which he rarely looked at, and a manila envelope, nothing but his name and the postage, and he paused on the back steps and tore at the flap to get at the contents. Department of Health Services at the very top. Wisconsin Marriage Certificate Application in large bold letters underneath. A man's name first, Mark Edward Edmonds. Then a woman's. Lena Renée Van Hagen.

Chapter 20

It had to be a mistake. She would have said something. Maybe there was another woman from Wisconsin with the same name, maybe she filed for the license but never actually got married, maybe she did get married but was divorced. He checked the form again, and saw that the date of marriage was a little more than a year ago.

It wasn't bullshit, it couldn't be, there were signatures and dates and stamps. He immediately checked for the guy's name online and found a little story on the featured celebrations section of the *Grand River Press* from a small town outside Milwaukee. He and Lena standing together, cheek to cheek, on the steps of a church, with the wooden doors of the sanctuary visible behind them. She beamed, her hair swept back and resplendent, the rich, amber curls looking dynamic against the cream fabric. Yes, she was beautiful, beautiful in the glossy, shimmering, toothy manner of all happy brides, but Blake could see, if he tried, the lack of commitment in her eyes, the dearth of true feeling. He tried to sketch a scenario in his mind for how she'd then ended up in Troy, in his life, but could only see lies from a fake do-gooder.

An opportune sign emerged, the daytime sky overhead turning darker and darker as he stood in the cold, and he hustled back to his apartment after grabbing the mail, a flurry of trembling thoughts racing through his mind. Someone wanted to hurt him. Someone wanted her gone from his life. He couldn't fathom anyone wanting to harm her, so he focused on the people in his world, the few who knew about Lena. And there weren't many, he might have mentioned her to his mom, to his sister and Amos at some point, perhaps to Tyner, but he couldn't remember. There wasn't a reason for anyone to mess with Blake, not about her.

He flipped open the computer, then slammed it closed. The TV was on but he ignored the basketball highlights, scrolled through the messages on his phone, the most recent from Lena, the old ones from Tyner, the terse orders from Clarke. Maybe it was her, sour about Blake leaving and never returning, jealous of a new girl, but he doubted she would have taken the time to do such arduous research and mail him an anonymous piece of evidence just to shit on his new relationship.

The photos, he suddenly thought. The pictures that were sent to him of Jessie and the kids, he'd never known who the culprit was, but he took a few minutes to think about everything that had transpired recently. The tragedy in Iona. Lena's later presence at the scene and at the funeral. The silver truck. The menacing freak outside Bochim who appeared, threatened him, and vanished. The texts. The fight outside the bar. Chris' revelation of Tyner's whereabouts on the night of the murders. The visit from the cops. The dead dog. Dead girls in Louisville. Crosses. Shoes. A fledgling romance. No matter how hard he tried, he couldn't connect any dots, couldn't find a reason for why all the events surrounding him had transpired, and he collapsed in his bed, unable to give anything more to the scattered remains of his mind.

He awoke to a decadent, emptying night and pawed his way to the bathroom, then cracked open the lone window and let the grievously cold air smash into him. An impulse hit him, a new one, to call Lena and spill his guts, but he knew she was working and couldn't talk. There was nothing for him to fall back on, no one to talk to, and the impulse died and left a crater he didn't know how to fill, other than his usual methods. He reheated some macaroni and cheese and engulfed it while he got dressed, then drove to Schwarz's and ordered an Old Fashioned. None of the usual drinkers were there, none that were familiar to him, and he steadied himself on his bar stool and let the complexity and darkness of the whiskey do its job while he tried to follow the game above him. The sweatshirt he chose seemed too small, the jeans too tight, he fidgeted and squirmed inside the clothes like his body was trying to find a place of comfort that was impossible to get to.

Another Old Fashioned, he wanted to tell Casey, but decided to switch to a beer, a less potent option, and thought about how Lena's life had led her to Troy and to him. If she was married, still, then the guy, Mark, was nowhere to be found, and she had no qualms about leaning into the tender and tumultuous world of Blake, so he had to give her that. He had to give her a chance to explain.

Half the Blue Moon stared at him from behind the brown glass, he left it there, tossed Casey the remainder of his cash and walked to the car. First a quick drive past Lena's, if she's home and awake, he thought, I'll talk to her and attempt to suss out what the hell's happening. The sounds of old-school rock hit him from the radio, a gnarly swirl of serrated guitars that sounded familiar, but he didn't have the classics catalogue memorized and waited until the DJ told the audience it was an Aerosmith staple. No sign of her car at the house and no lights other than a blinding motion sensor above the front door that must have had a 20-foot range, so he kept moving, headed to the hospital even though he knew not to bother her there. He parked far away from the emergency entrance, kept the engine on but cut the music. The person who sent the marriage certificate knew about him and Lena. The person who sent him the pictures knew he had a connection to Tyner. The other frivolities, the seeming coincidences, were just that, and he had to ignore them and think about the contact, the one infiltrating his life. He needed help from Amos.

A text seemed inappropriate, given the heaviness of what he needed, but as it was nearing 10 o'clock and he knew both Amos and Landa were early risers, it would have to suffice. "Hey Amos, I've had some odd contacts recently, related to what's been happening with the mess up in Iona, wondering if you can do a little digging and try to find out who's behind it. Thx." He tapped send, drove home, hoping his tone was clear in the quick digital missive.

That night, snowflakes plummeted out of the sky and accumulated in mountainous drifts and packed the roadsides in craggy mounds. Amos drove slowly and looked at his phone, saw another message from Landa and typed out a reply: "Love you, too, see you in the morning." She always checked in with him when he worked late shifts, even though she struggled to stay awake past 9:30 and her messages were often gibberish that he didn't bother to decipher and usually responded to without even reading. He'd left the highway 20 minutes earlier and delved deeper into Hudson County, scanning the road and the roadsides for issues and hoping he wouldn't have to get out of his car. The cold troubled him, it always had, he grew up in Bowling Green, in western Kentucky, and never had to deal with the kind of ice and snow pummeling him all winter on the other side of the Ohio.

He drove slowly, savoring his time in the car, pushed uphill into the area surrounding Bochim, he didn't know the place well but rarely noticed anything amiss when he cruised along the empty roads in his patrol vehicle. Big mailboxes, barns and large white outbuildings, sloping yards dotted with small ponds and plastic deer and bathtub Mary's. He'd never understood those shrines and asked Landa what the deal was, and she quickly filled him in on the Catholic history of the area and the veneration of Mary. But he'd always been a good Baptist boy, and no matter how many times he saw them sprouting out of a lawn he just shook his head in quiet disbelief.

A squawk came over his radio, dispatch reported a call about a tree blocking part of Nebraska Road, which turned into State Road 338 before it left Hudson County, and he responded that he'd check it out. The gravel lot of an abandoned carpet store appeared, and he turned around slowly and headed east, past Crystalville, Irish Creek, Hidden Hive, and Chicken Place, none of which were towns or even blips of a town, just points on the map comprising a house or church or dilapidated business. The asphalt curved to the north and he spotted a split, 338 going north and another road, 65, branching to the east, and he stayed on 338, past a large grassy lot stuffed with farm equipment, a sign advertising a daycare center next to a driveway leading deep to a ranch house, and an endless expanse of trees and woods and forest, every branch and pine needle and knob of earth speckled with bright white snow.

The limb appeared as the road rose in elevation a couple of degrees, and he pulled up and cut the engine but kept the headlights illuminated. Outside, the wind swirled and tossed stinging pellets at his face, and he squinted and turned his head against the gale and moved to the front of his car. Thick, veiny wood stared at him, and he used his boot to roll against the limb and test its weight, figuring the size and length and amount of snow would make it too difficult to move on his own. But he bent down and tried anyway, hefting against the log with what little traction he could get in the hard snow, using his wiry frame to push as much as he could, but the limb barely got going and refused to roll at all. He'd need some help, but there was no telling how long it would take to arrive, and he was bored just at the thought of sitting in his car for 30 minutes or an hour.

A crackle of sound caught his attention, something dry and heavy, and he twisted his head a little to see behind him, at the sliver of trees that abutted a steep embankment and led downhill to another empty county road. Nothing. An engine, tires on the road, far away, too far to be seen. Amos kept looking, rubbed his hands together, his state-issued gloves not enough to properly combat the arctic air mass surrounding him.

The blow struck from the side, clubbed him in the rib cage, and Amos crumpled to the ground, moaning and reaching for his gun, but his hands groped nothing but snow. "Whhhhooooooo," he started, but a heavy boot slammed into his midsection and he doubled over and coughed and retched and tried to roll on his side to avoid catching more shots to the gut.

"That's enough," a man's flinty voice intoned from nearby, and Amos peeked out of the corner of his eye, and saw a small shadow. Then another shadow, taller, with a large, square head, blonde, beady eyes of sharp blue, a fierce grimace, a long, heavy object, some kind of club, in his hand. The voice said something else, the wind grabbed it and swept it away, just as the second shadow lifted his arm, and smashed the club into Amos' skull.

Chapter 21

No one knocked at his place, never, but he heard it from somewhere in his unconsciousness, lifted out of bed and moved slowly to the door, listened, heard the light pounding again, and opened the door to see what was up. "Hello?" he called into the emptiness of the garage, and heard a muffled voice call his name. "Hello, mom?" he said again, then realized with a start that the voice belonged to Lena. "Hold on a sec!" he shouted, rushed upstairs to grab a long-sleeve shirt and ran his hand through his hair to smooth out any knots or kinks that had formed while he slept.

"Hey, what're you doing here," he said as he opened the door and ushered her inside the garage.

"Nothing. I mean, I wanted to see you, and I just got off and figured I'd come by." She looked like she'd gotten off work, hair pulled back, no makeup, sweatpants, and a puffed-up navy blue hoodie with a University of Illinois-Chicago logo. He pointed the way and she walked up the stairs with him trailing, noting the heavy black Teva boots that still had bits of snow clinging to the side, but she took them off before going in and left them at the top step. She kept shedding garments, dropping the big hooded sweatshirt on a chair, pulling off a white long-sleeved shirt and dumping it on the floor, yanking off her long socks that had comically large stripes wrapped around the calves, and pulling down her black leggings until she was clad in just muted pink underwear and a skimpy black tank top.

"Just wanted to come by, huh?" he asked, and walked slowly over to the bed.

They lay together, and Blake felt light, all light, sweeping over him. And for the first time he realized his need for love was a real thing. Not that he loved Lena, or that she loved him, they weren't there yet and were mature enough to recognize that while that was definitely on the horizon, they weren't in those depths yet. But what he felt for her, what his body was telling him, what his brain was screaming at him, was that he needed that kind of closeness and intimacy. That tenderness, that longing, that focus he gave to every moment, was so far removed from the blatant and forged machinations he'd used on his previous relationships. And he knew it was the best thing that had ever happened to him.

"What's on your mind?" he asked her, it wasn't terribly original or deep, but he wanted to talk, the envelope with the evidence pointing to her marriage was still on his mind, but his mood was inquisitive rather than accusative. He just wanted to know what was going on.

"I don't know," she said with a sigh, and rolled from her back to her side, her body curling into him and her hand gripping his biceps. "That this isn't what I imagined, that being with you isn't what I intended, but it feels right. It makes me giddy because it feels like home, like I belong with you, and it's making my heart tremble and my head spin."

"Uh huh," he murmured, and leaned over to kiss her forehead. "I know what you mean, I'm feeling the same thing. Even though there's some shit pulling at us, and there always will be, I can tell what you mean to me already, cause I'd crawl through miles of this frozen waste just to get a look at you, to see your eyes and to see your smile."

A smile broke out on her face, a big one, but then it dissipated a little and she looked straight up, into the ceiling he'd painted himself in high school at his dad's behest. "What's pulling at us?"

"I mean, you know, just the endless shit of life, all the drudgery and responsibilities we have. The good stuff, too," he said, not wanting to lump in his picayune life with the admirable way she functioned every day. "I didn't know how to bring this up, I didn't know if I should bring it up, but I got something in the mail recently. Really weird, honestly, that I got this, but it looks legit. A marriage certificate, with your name on it."

"A what?"

"Well, I got an envelope in the mail the other day, and there was a copy of a marriage certificate inside. Some guy named Mark Edmonds on the groom line, and you on the bride's. But it's OK, I figured it was something you didn't want to bring up, and I'm honestly cool with whatever is going on, I'm not here to judge or anything."

"Wait, wait, wait a minute," she said, sitting up in the bed, and yanking at the sheet to cover herself. "Someone mailed you a marriage certificate? With my name on it?"

"Yes, and it was really weird, because there have been a lot of incidents recently that I can't explain. Texts and emails and other shit, and then the envelope with the certificate. But I don't care, you know, about what happened in your past, your marriage, I'm ready for devotion, for a dutiful life. With you."

She scrunched the sheet in her hands, ready to pounce, but stopped herself, and refocused her gaze on him. "Yeah, it's true, I was married. Actually, I am married."

"You are? You mean still, right now?"

"I got married 18 months ago, but I didn't know he, Mark, was an addict. Drugs, pills, heroin," she said with a look of remorse. "Two weeks after the wedding he went berserk, and I had to lock him out and call the police. I thought he'd go to rehab and try to save the marriage, but he bailed and took the car and emptied our shared account and disappeared, and I took the rest of the money, filed a restraining order, went to my parents' and waited for him to turn up. He never did, and I finally went to a lawyer and tried to start the process of getting a divorce.

"Then I got the job down here and had to leave before everything got finalized with the courts. I haven't seen him or talked to him in over a year, but when he finally turns up and hopefully signs the paperwork, it'll all be over."

"Damn, that's just, wow, that's terrible So you mean you had no idea about him, your ex? Doing drugs and everything?"

"No, he's one of those people who can hide their addiction and their behavior pretty well. Fooled me from the get-go, it turned out."

"Oh, yeah, I know what you mean," he said. "Look, I'm sorry to spring this on you, make you feel confronted, it was just so jarring to see that after it came in the mail. I know those kinds of memories and feelings can really drag you down emotionally."

"It's OK, God knows I've dealt with so much shit in the last couple of years."

More things came to his mind, more to say to ease Lena's mind, but the phone rang and he reached for it, saw his sister's name and frowned. She rarely called him. Never, really, just a text every now and then. And the time, it was a little past eight in the morning, and the thought of her reaching out made him wary of finding out what was going on.

"Hang on," he said to Lena, then swiped the call open. "Hello, Landa, what's up?"

"They found him up there, Blake, they found him," she sputtered, her voice shrill and piercing through the phone's speaker.

"What? Found who, where?"

"Amos, he was gone all night, didn't check in with his supervisor, didn't respond when they tried to radio him and call him, they found him up in the county by that place, all beat to shit. He's in the hospital, come here, please, Blake, please."

"All right, I'm coming," he said, then hung up and hurriedly grabbed clothes strewn on the floor.

"What's wrong?" Lena asked as he dressed.

"My brother-in-law, he's in the hospital, the emergency room, I guess, he got attacked or something last night." He got his clothes on, looked for his keys, and realized she was still on the bed, still naked except for her underwear, and he took a few seconds to gather himself. "Um, stay, take as long as you need, get some sleep, whatever. I'll call you, you know, when I figure out what's happening."

"I'll come with, give me a minute."

"No, no, it's fine, I'll be fine."

"Come on, Blake," she said, and reached for her clothes on the floor.

"I'm serious. We'll be fine, we got this." He started for the door, not giving her a chance to respond or come with, and hustled down the steps and out to his car, wishing he had time to allow himself to be comforted, but he couldn't do it, not then, and not with his sister and likely his mom waiting there.

Without waiting for the engine to warm up, he churned out of his spot and tore through the streets, arrived at the hospital in less than 10 minutes and jogged as carefully as he could to the emergency department, almost skipped past triage but stopped and asked to go back and see Amos. "The cop, he's my brother-in-law," he threw in, just in case there was an issue with the nurse denying him entry. Under her blue headband he could see her brown hair pulled back and tinged with green dye, and a pink tattoo in the shape of a tree or flower peeked out from her left biceps, but she moved with a studious bearing, and ushered him to a room not far from where he'd gotten his head treated.

A bevy of cops and official-looking hospital personnel stood around in the hall, talking with one another quietly with arms folded, and Blake slid into the frame, trying to make eye contact with someone who'd recognize him. The nurse, though, ushered him through the crowd, explaining who he was, knocked on the door for him. "Landa," he said when he pushed through the door, and saw her sitting next to the elevated bed, her hair wispy and sticking out from a wrap that she probably never let another soul, other than Amos, see her in.

"I'm trying not to lose it, B, I'm trying," she said, and rubbed her hand across her eyes. He stepped close to her, she hadn't called him B in years, and he suddenly felt the closeness that had been missing between them for so long. "How could this kinda thing happen here, to him, to us? An ambush in the middle of nowhere, are you kidding me?"

"He got ambushed? By who?"

"They don't know, he got a call about a tree or something in the road up by that freaky place, the one you kept bothering him about. And he got out of the car and got clubbed with a bat, something heavy, and hard." She pointed to Amos, whose head had been bandaged and wrapped and had specks of blood peeking through. "He's lucky he's alive, someone found him in the snow by his car, got him inside to warm up and then drove down the hill so he could get picked up by the ambulance."

"Goddamn, I can't believe it."

"Don't swear, Blake, please."

"I think some cuss words are fine, your husband got his head busted open, he damn near got killed, you can say whatever you want."

"No matter what, we stay positive, we pray and we get through whatever God puts in front of us."

"OK."

"Besides, you were the one putting all that nonsense in his head about that place, about the bodies of those girls, he spent so much time looking up things for you and tracking people and searching on his computer. This has something to do with you and that place, I know it."

"Come on, this had nothing to do with me or what happened to Jessie. He was on duty, and you said there was a tree down. Some asshole just hates cops or something, that's it."

"No, it was you, you almost got him killed." She buried her face in her hands, and Blake stepped away, winced, thought about Uncle Joe's words about Nelson killing the brother he'd never known about. He'd tried to find some evidence, a story or an obituary or some note online about the child or the accident, but there was nothing, and he wondered if Joe, in his end-of-life delirium, had made the whole thing up or confused his father with someone else. When he called Meena to talk to Joe and try to get more information, she said, matter-of-factly, that he wasn't able to talk, and wasn't sure if he ever would again.

"Listen, Yolanda, I promise I never expected anything like this to happen to Amos. He's a good guy, and a good cop, and the only reason I've been talking to him about that is because I know something is going on, something happened to Jessie, someone did something to her, they caused her and the kids to die out there, and I needed help to try and figure it all out.

"And now I know I need to do something to finish this."

Chapter 22

First there was the Harmony Society, a group of eight hundred Pietists originally from Württemberg, Germany, who left Pennsylvania and arrived on the banks of the Wabash River in western Indiana in the early 1800s. Their account of utopia, as envisioned by founder George Rapp and organized by his adopted son, Frederick, would allow for everyone in the society to achieve worldly success and happiness through education, hard work, and ingenuity. For 10 years, the community operated as a self-sustained, hardscrabble town of productivity and religious perfection. Later, after the Rapps soured on Indiana and wanted to uproot the society, a Scottish industrialist named Robert Owen purchased the town of New Harmony, intending to transform the initial vision into an even greater society, one that would create a newer, better world through Owen's ideals of social reform. The new town, referred to as a Community of Equality in an updated Constitution that outlined the average citizen's day-to-day functions, crumbled under the lack of leadership, an influx of layabouts, a lack of skilled workers, and numerous conflicts between people who struggled to reconcile the ideals of the society with the inequality that governed their daily lives.

After that, the communes, later referred to as intentional communities, emerged during the 1960s and 70s in central and southern Indiana, none with the depth or the reach of New Harmony, but they attracted their share of divinely inspired personalities, hippies, nature lovers, counterculture figures, storytellers, gardeners, carpenters, stoners, artists, and scoundrels. Needmore, situated among the bucolic forests and ridges of Brown County, grew to more than a dozen permanent homes and nearly 100 residents, who enjoyed the freedom of living a life of self-reliance on land purchased by wealthy partners Larry and Kathy Canada. A small band of 20-somethings purchased 304 acres in Monroe County, outside Bloomington, and started May Creek Farm in 1976, hoping to survive on aquaculture, tofu making, and selling crafts and other handmade goods. They lived in teepees, drove miles to acquire fresh water, and chipped in to handle the backbreaking labor of maintaining its unpaved road and its numerous communal structures.

Padanaram, also called God's Valley, was created by a prophet and preacher named Daniel Wright, who halted his travels in Martin County and found the perfect spot for his own utopia in a typical pocket of conservatism in southern Indiana. The area surrounding his valley was replete with churches of many stripes, all of them heavy on scripture and piety and being saved and giving yourself totally and completely to God. And giving yourself to the leader of the community. The kids who grew up in God's Valley swam in the lake and chased after dogs and ate lunches together and rode ponies. Adults shared property and taxes and food and childcare and worshiped together in communal spaces and lived off the profits from their lumber mill, but when business slowed and Daniel Wright passed, the community modernized as much as it could, and people got regular jobs, sent their kids to public schools, and spent time in the pub that had been built on the property to have beers and commiserate about the world.

Blake drove, and thought, and couldn't explain any of it, couldn't connect the strange worlds around him with the scandalous events that had occurred, and his head swam as he listened to Lowell George warble, "You might say you ain't got a hold on yourself," and he turned the music off and let the car move in silence, looked at the caked-over streets, the salted tires and undercarriages and dirty frames of the other vehicles surrounding him. Schwarz's drew his attention, the mouth-watering burn of bourbon called out like never before, and he stopped and went inside, every seat and stool empty, the bartender, someone other than Casey, sitting and playing with his phone. "Hey, Elijah neat, please. And some water," he said, sat, and absorbed a mouthful of warm, sweet whiskey, swallowed it with his eyes closed. Those communities, the one's he'd read about, weren't the same as Bochim, even Padanaram seemed to have shifted to a sleepy little village that happened to have originated with a charismatic visionary. Who are these people, he thought, these Bochimites, and determined, as the empty glass hit the counter, that he needed to go to the liquor store. He needed a whole bottle. He needed time to think, the only way he knew how.

When he unscrunched his eyes in the dark of the early evening, he reached across his body to feel for her, but she was gone. The night felt blacker than ever, sometimes the light pollution from Louisville emitted an eerie yellow glow that brightened even the darkest of Troy City nights, but as Blake looked out his window, he saw nothing.

What is this pain, he thought as he fumbled for his phone, attempting to make out the numbers on the little screen. 6:05, he could barely read it, didn't understand how he'd been asleep long enough to pass through the late morning, the afternoon, to miss the diluted sunset and cross directly into the burnt crust of the night. Didn't know why his brain reared back and smashed into his skull every few seconds and sent him to his knees. He'd left the hospital, he remembered, after promising his sister he'd keep Amos away from whatever he had planned, and drove back to his apartment. Or did I, he thought, slowly realizing he had no memory after he left the bar, couldn't recall speaking with Lena about what happened to Amos, or his mom, or eating, or arriving back at his place.

For a few seconds he felt around on his body, searching for something unusual to explain what had wiped out his recollection of the previous day, but nothing seemed out of place, and he sat up and tried to scan the room for anything to snatch at his attention hunted for a clue with his eyes, but gave up because of the pain. The phone. He looked again, his eyes finally focusing, saw the time that his sister had called in the morning, 8:12, saw calls from his mom and Lena in the log, even spotted a text from Tyner that he'd apparently read that said, "sorry bout Amos."

He looked up at the ceiling, at the cedar planks his dad had run along the edges to mimic the effect of crown molding. A pang hit him, hunger, and he nearly bent over in discomfort as it increased in intensity. Food, such a distant thought, and he pored through his head to pick up the remnants of what his last meal looked or tasted like. Nothing.

A niggling little thought stayed with him, and he swiped across his screen again, found the calendar, the dates, went back to the call logs, the texts, back and forth, until he almost slapped himself in disbelief at what he was seeing. One day. He'd been asleep, unconscious, or had completely forgotten, an entire day. Twenty-four hours. Lena's visit, the rush to the hospital, the talk with Landa, all had come the day before, and he had no clue how everything, every minute and every moment, had disappeared.

I know how to handle my liquor, he thought, I know what my limits are. He began a search of his small apartment, hunting for anything to explain why he couldn't remember a damn thing. The bottle, that had to be it, and he skulked into the kitchen, half-bent over, to seek it out, see how much he'd consumed. It winked at him from the counter, next to the fridge, the glimmering clear glass with the rich brown liquid inside so shiny and innocent there, clearly he had only had a few drinks, maybe three, maybe four, but not enough to place him in the kind of stupor that eliminated a day of brain activity.

She might have been working, but he called Lena, she had to know he hadn't abandoned her, left her alone in his bed and then ignored her phone calls like a dipshit. That wasn't him, she likely knew that, but she had to hear it out of his mouth.

"Lena, hi, I'm sorry it's been so long," he said into her voice mail after she failed to pick up. "Something happened to me after I left from the hospital, I'm not really sure how time got away from me like it did, and my head is pounding, my body is wracked with pain, feels like I've been drugged or something. Call me, please, when you can." He hung up, and looked at the little table in his combined living room and bedroom and office and closet and gym and dining room and bar. Under a copy of the *Atlantic* he'd bought months earlier when he was at a bookstore in Louisville, he spotted the vape pen. Couldn't have been that, he thought, a couple of puffs never led to anything but giddiness and sleepiness. But he picked it up and stared at the silver shaft, the clear bulb of oil, the white tip, and tried to envision what he'd done the day before. Got home with the bourbon, the cheap Evan Williams that tasted good on ice, and sat with a drink while he pored over the facts, the details, the pictures, the nuance of all that had occurred. He'd taken the pen and grabbed a couple of pulls, just enough to relax his mind and his body and let his thoughts run wild without interference. And then he lost the thread of the rest of the day.

The pen, the weed, the oil, the smoke, something in there had affected him. Just like the booze, it shouldn't have happened, he never indulged to the point of passing out or losing a sense or where or when he was. It didn't make sense.

"Mom, you there?" he said into the phone. They hadn't talked about Amos, not that he could remember, and he felt like he needed to get in touch, to reforge the bond they once had, and to try to keep their little family going any way he could. Their demonstrations of affection had withered to nothing, and at times it felt to Blake like they treated one another like landlord and tenant. There were no theatrics to their relationship, just a defection of love going back to Nelson's death and Blake's return home from Ohio State. "Mom, how's Amos? What's new, has he regained consciousness?"

"Blake. Where are you?" Marianna asked, her voice echoing slightly.

"Home, I'm in the apartment. Why?"

"We've just been wondering where you've been. You haven't answered your phone, your car's not there, and all your lights have been off for two days."

"My car?" He went to the window and looked to the street, no sign of the Camry, and pushed the phone harder into his ear. "No,

I'm here, I just had, I got sick or something, I haven't felt alright since yesterday afternoon. So is he OK?"

"Yes, he's stable, the bleeding in his head has been stopped, but he's still unconscious. And they decided he didn't need to be transferred to a neuro unit in Louisville."

"Well, good, thank goodness. Are the cops looking around in Bochim trying to find out who did that to him? Tracking the phone call that led him there in the first place?"

"They went up and talked to some people, but there were no witnesses, and the call came from a farm house nearby, an elderly couple's house. They don't really know anything right now."

"Really? Nothing? Someone up there did that to him, I know it, there's been too much going on, too much death and destruction."

"I don't know, Blake, that's what the captain told us at the hospital."

"Shit." He sat down, then got up again, unable to resolve the tension that roiled his insides and left him unable to really talk to his mom.

"Just stay home, get yourself better. We'll take care of Amos and call you if we need anything. Hang out with your friend and take it easy."

"My friend? Who, Tyner?"

"No, your new, I don't know, friend, girlfriend, whatever."

"How do you know about her?"

"She came out of your apartment yesterday morning, I saw her when I came back home to get some stuff for Landa before I went to the hospital." She paused, and Blake heard a voice from the hospital room coming quietly through the speakers. "Seems like a very sweet person. Listen, Blake, I need to go, I hope you feel better soon."

"Mom, hang on a sec," he started, but she'd already tapped the end call button, apparently. Blake looked at his phone, wanting to call Lena again, to capture and feel her essence in the little quirks of her voice, to skip the gradual road to love and sweep into her as fast as he possibly could. But she hadn't answered, and he needed to talk.

"Landa, listen, don't hang up," he said quickly, hoping his mom was still there and would overhear him.

"OK."

"Talk to the captain again, tell him what Amos has been up to, tell him about Bochim and everything I've been texting him and emailing him. They'll believe you."

"Blake, I'm trying to be careful here, trying to support Amos. I don't want to get his bosses angry by asking them too many questions or accusing them of not doing their jobs."

"It's not about accusing them, sis, just get them to go back up there and talk to the leader, or somebody, anybody, they know something. They did something."

"I need to go, Blake.."

"Wait, wait. What did mom say about Lena, where'd she go after she left my place?"

"Who? Blake, I gotta go. Bye" She hung up and left him clutching the phone, unable to articulate that he suddenly felt an instinctual fear for what was going to happen to Lena.

Chapter 23

Blake wanted to call, again, to drive by her house, look for the little black Volkswagen, scurry to the hospital, if necessary, and hope to spot the car and punt all his fears outside himself and return his focus to Jessie and Bochim. He wanted to believe, like all the overachievers and ambitious people he'd encountered, that she customarily and expectantly poured everything she had into work, hoping to eradicate her inadequacies or insecurities or sadness with more and more time spent helping people. Mostly, though, he just wanted to believe she was OK. Because if she wasn't, then it was his fault, and it would be his responsibility to ensure her pain was undone.

But instead he stayed put, stayed still, and opened the computer to write and unburden his blazing, saintly thoughts. "What I see all around me this lengthy, evil winter, is that everything has changed. The menace of death and destruction has penetrated Troy and Hudson County and my life, and it's got to stop. I may not be the one, other people and institutions need to flex their muscles and investigate, indict, subpoena, arrest, thwart, anything to stop the brazen reign of terror conducted by the person or persons who have killed young girls, killed families, killed children, and thrown every aspect of this little world into hell."

The words flowed, and the emotion, and the reprimands, and the despair of someone who feels they have no choice in what was to come, and he sent it all into the cavernous collection of black, blinking servers that comprised the Internet. His logic, his plan, had begun to emerge as he'd typed, and he ran it over in his head, the snarled mess of deviating paths and intentions bashing into one another so violently that he had to cover his head in a pillow and eliminate every distraction. All the noise, all the light. He had to dwell in darkness for what was unsayable, and likely undoable, to eventually burst forth with the truth.

The house stood blank and alone, and Blake waited for a few seconds in his car, desperate to get out but chained by fear. He rummaged in his coat pocket, felt for the slim bottle of Evan Williams he'd stuck in there the previous day, and took a healthy swig. Only then did he emerge from the car and head to the front door. Tyner opened it quickly, seconds after Blake knocked. He stepped back to allow Blake inside, and the two friends, former friends, stood and looked at one another, each with eyes clouded by what they'd lost. But Blake moved forward, ready to tell Tyner what he needed.

"Whoever it is, and I think I might know who, he's coming after me now. And I have to go stop it all, so I need your piece."

"My what?"

"Your piece, your nine."

"Nah, man, I don't have that anymore. Jessie had me get rid of it when Jaz was born. She thought," he started, then dropped his head a little, paused with his eyes closed. "She thought it was too dangerous to have a gun with kids in the house."

"Oh. Shit. I gotta find somebody, then. Maybe Chris Blaine, he knows people, knows how to get things."

"Blake, you can't do that."

"Look, I have to go up there, to Bochim, I think Lena was taken, or they know what happened to her, because I've called her, she's not at home, she's not at work. And if I have some protection I'll feel better going up there by myself."

"What about the cops?"

"My sister said they already went and talked to people up there and don't have any evidence that anyone was involved, and I have no proof they did anything to her. Just a feeling."

"There's gotta be another way. Lean on the cops some more, call a reporter, a TV journalist from Louisville, get some news coverage and then maybe the police will hit 'em harder."

"It ain't gonna work, man. I gotta go there, see it all for myself. I have to make a contribution to this fight."

"Listen, B. You don't have to do anything. You're not a superhero or a soldier or anything. You're just a guy, and it's not on you to fix something so massive."

The tension tethered the two to one another, and Blake sought a chair behind him, a plush blue thing with no arms that he'd sat in while he held baby Georgy in his arms a year earlier. Blake wasn't the most sensitive guy in the world, he had enough self-awareness to see that in himself, but the incessant danger that had fled into his life left him without the filters of the past, and he barreled ahead with what he'd had on his mind for weeks. "Hey, T, when did you know?"

"Know what?"

"When did you know you liked men? When did it hit you, when did you act on it?"

Tyner didn't say anything, he retreated to his own seat, his long legs, the indestructible trail blazers that had once seemed destined to lead him to greatness, pressed into the glass table in front of him. "I don't know, man," he said quietly. "Back in the day, we used to cut grass in the summer, you remember, dragged that red push mower through your neighborhood looking to make some money. Used to clear about $30 a week, each. One time you were gone for a month or something, went to Germany with your mom and sister, and I worked by myself. There was a lady you never met, her house was over by that chair factory down on 18th street, and she let me mow her yard and bag the grass and trim her edges for $10 a week. She showed me her weed eater and gas cans in the garage that first time and then let me be, and I'd go in there to take a break and grab a drink, she had a yellow fridge stocked with bottled water and drinks and said I could take whatever I wanted.

"The last time I went, right before you got back, it started to drizzle while I was mowing, so I went in the garage to wait it out. She had boxes everywhere, stuffed with junk and old clothes and books and dolls, all kinds of shit. I pulled one over to me from where I was sitting, thought it had comic books or magazines in it, and when I dug down in there were nudie mags. But, like, it was all men. Naked men. Sometimes more than one, together, touching each other. I dropped it, at first, then couldn't help myself and looked at one, then another, then I was digging through other boxes looking for more. I couldn't stop, and I was overwhelmed, and ashamed, and excited, and the fire and temptation in me was too much, and I huddled in a corner and rubbed one out so hard and so quick that I was just disgusted with myself. And I took off and never went back there.

"You don't understand, B, when you play ball, when you become a big deal like I was, the girls, man, it's insane. They waited for me outside the gym after games, they offered me rides home and let me drive their SUV's, they bought me clothes, they brought their girlfriends into my dorm room and told me to pick who was the hottest, then they'd double-team me. All the shit I used to tell you about, that was just the tip of the iceberg."

"For real?"

"Yeah, but I knew the whole time. I knew it in Philly, when I went to a club with a friend from campus. I knew it here when I was with Jessie and I'd go to the spot in Louisville. And I played it like I was with other girls cause I figured that wouldn't be as bad. And that wasn't fair to her, and it's a fucking tragedy that I had to have my kids taken from me. But I'm here, I'm ready to do right, and I can't be down with what you're trying to do."

"So that's it, you're just gonna let those freaks up there get away with their evil shit and not do a goddamn thing?"

"Look, I know about the people up there. Jessie told me stories through the years about them, about how they behaved and operated. There are some strange folks up there, yeah, but there's also some really dangerous people, too," Tyner said. "They have secrets, lots of secret places and passages and buildings and people, they tried to hide things from her, lied about who she was, what her purpose was. I'm gonna leave them alone and let that place destroy itself, whether it takes a day or a year or a decade. And you should, too."

"Well, gun or no, I can't. I can't just sit here in Troy and wait for anyone or anything."

"Blake, wait," Tyner said, and turned around, walked over to a cabinet against the wall and opened a drawer. He came back with a small wooden semi-circle in his palm, and handed it to Blake. "This is small, you can conceal it somewhere, don't trust a soul when you get up there, and be careful."

Blake looked at the little piece of wood and noticed the sliver of metal sticking out, and unfolded a curved blade, slightly dull with age but still sharp enough to do damage. "What's this?"

"It was my granddaddy's, he used to hunt down in Alabama where he grew up, and used this skinning knife on deer and raccoons and shit. Keep it. Keep it hidden, and protect yourself, B." The quiet whoosh of air rushing out of the floor vents provided the only sound, and the two stared at one another for a few seconds, realizing that their friendship had been pushed long enough and hard enough for them to finally erase the dark, miserable nothingness it had become. They'd never be boys again, but they could be there for each other.

"Thanks, Tyner." Blake went out to his Camry, opened an app, and typed out three words before hitting send: "On my way."

Chapter 24

The walk to the temple took nearly 30 minutes, and he went immediately. He'd been summoned, and he always obeyed. Traipsing along the covered path, he spotted the lingering detritus of the plots long abandoned by non-believers. A camper, crushed by the weight of an oak, that had once been used as temporary housing for a home that never got built. Rusted houseboats that hadn't seen water in decades. A red Ford Bronco nearly swallowed by the earth, its tires long buried beneath grass and dirt and rocks. Farm equipment and trailers and wood sheds and greenhouses turned to relics, glass broken out and wood rotted and metal deteriorated by oxygen and wind and water. Small pallets of brick and cinder blocks half-covered by shredded tarps. The neglect bothered him, he'd said many times to many people that they needed to project resilience and prosperity, from every corner of the land and from every member of the community. But the projects he proposed remained unfulfilled, and vast swaths of pristine acreage remained untouched or sullen with rust and carelessness.

A walkway emerged, cleared with a shovel and dusted with a broom to reveal the flat stones laid out and leading to the entrance. He used to go once a day, no matter the weather; swampy heat, crushing cold, downpours, assertive wind, delightful cool, the trek happened regardless, and he listened intently to instructions, or advice, or stories, and carried out whatever task was laid before him.

There was no door, just a tall opening covered with a buffalo hide hung from the stony frame and a series of three tight turns built to keep out the precipitation and force the believers to navigate one final trial of obedience: follow him, no matter what.

He went in, expecting to find the usual scene: a hand-carved wooden chair, its back forged into a giant cross, occupied by the wizened but still formidable presence of the guardian of the temple, the patriarch of Bochim, the Ecclesiast, Bezalel. He bent to a knee, lowered his head, and after five seconds rose and took his place on a small wooden bench. The rocky exterior gave way, inside, to ceilings of wide cedar planks, small arched windows, and the Great Room, where Bezalel spoke to all of the Bochim faithful twice a week. And to his most faithful servant, Eric, nearly every day.

The Camry shuddered and sputtered as it wound its way up the hills and into the depths of Hudson County. He tried to go silent, to drive from Tyner's to Bochim with no music, but he couldn't do it, he needed something to pump him up. He shuffled through songs on his phone, all the hypest R&B tracks he had, nearly turned it off, but came to the funkiest Funkadelic track he had and let it play. The deep, distorted spoken word verse gave way to piercing guitars and ethereal vocals, and Blake found himself nearly shaking with fear as he heard the narrator intone, "Death waited in the shadows."

The asphalt seemed clear, no snow had fallen in more than two days, and the county crews had been able to navigate their equipment and vehicles across all the major roads. Blake drove slowly, not wanting to attract unwanted attention from either the state police, who might still be patrolling the area, or anyone from Bochim. The trees eased past the passenger window, the same pines and elms and hickories and beeches that held the handful of geodes he'd seen on his previous trip. He continued another mile, maybe more, the landscape identical from second to second, and wondered if the entrance to the community was hidden from the main road somehow.

A pair of stones, beige creek stones, the tops craggy and uneven, the sides spiky and serrated, caught his eye. They weren't tall, or shiny, or obvious in any way, but he spotted them, their presence on either side of a flatter, lower patch of snow made him pull to the side. Enough room for a car, he thought, gauging the distance between the two trees propping up the stones and the empty tract behind. No tire tracks or marks of any kind, but he couldn't dismiss the idea: Lena was back there.

A moment with his eyes closed, and he turned the car in the other direction, drove a little way until he could settle the Camry in an out of the way spot off to the side. Swallowed another dose of whiskey, then walked back to the two stones, and pressed forward, into the woods, and felt the indentations of gravel under the soles of his black Under Armour's. A road. He wanted to continue on but stopped, swept through the snow to his right and began to move through the woods, slow but determined. Sticks and twigs and limbs snapped and popped despite his best efforts to creep through silently, and he followed the path as best as he could, expecting a non-stop plummet deeper into the forest. But after just 10 minutes he came around a curve and saw the beginnings of what he suspected was Bochim.

A small house, just a white box, really, stood by itself amidst the packed snow, a plume of smoke curling out of the chimney and a twinkle of light peeping from a front window. Nothing stirred, no dog barked, no engine roared to life, and Blake crept on, hoping to find something or someone more tangible to approach. A long building loomed in the near distance, with a couple of cars sitting out front, their hoods and roofs and trunks covered in white, a couple of picnic tables close by, also covered in snow, and a tall metal shed in the back. The building looked like a meeting place of sorts, with large open windows exposing long tables and a kitchen and a carpeted area dotted with small chairs. He moved closer, clenched his hands inside his black gloves, felt in his pocket for the props he'd brought along, and knocked on the door.

"Good morning, Ecclesiast. Are you warm enough? Would you like some tea or another blanket?"

"No, son, the warmth of the temple is enough for me today. Have you considered what I offered you the other day?"

"I have, Bezalel. But I'm, I don't know, not sure how it's supposed to work. She hasn't talked to me in years, she has abandoned us and is a Chronicler in name only. Your sons have maintained the truth and traditions of Bochim, not her."

"You're right," Bezalel said in a soft voice, which came out in nearly a whisper at times but always thundered through the temple during times of congregation. "But things have changed for her. She has a son, and she is no longer living in her home. She needs us, her family, more than ever. My son has reached out to her, and she has agreed to meet with me to discuss a way for them to come back to us, but I believe in what God has shown me. You and her will be together, you will become the next Ecclesiast, and you shall lead Bochim, with my daughter at your side."

"If you've seen this, then I'll do as you say." Eric shifted on the bench, his legs suddenly twitchy and his body starting to rock a little.

"You see, I will make a man of you. You've tried to invent yourself, to be somebody else, to no avail. But I've believed in you, in who you are meant to be. Trust me."

"Yes, I will."

A dragging, thundering discomfort hammered him in his gut, but Blake stood still, waiting for someone to answer. A creak, the door slid back and a woman stood in the frame, small and slender and gray-haired and kind-eyed, and Blake raised a hand in greeting and smiled.

"Hi, how are you?"

"I'm well. Please, come in out of the cold," the woman said, and moved aside to let him enter.

"Thanks, thank you. I was wondering," Blake said, pulling his pen and little notebook out of his coat pocket. "I'm writing a story about, well, about your community, and I was wondering if I could see, um, Eric?"

"I see. And what's your name, young man?"

"Oh, I'm sorry, it's Blake Prince. I live in Troy City."

"Ok." She moved backward, into a kitchen area, and grabbed a large wooden spoon, stuck it into a big bubbling stockpot and stirred. "Troy. Quite a place. I was born there."

"Yeah, it is. So is Eric around? I wasn't sure how to contact him so I just came up."

"You know, you are in a beautiful place. Not like Troy. Here, you are welcome in a community that is an example of how the world can flourish."

Blake stared, unsure how to react to the woman, to her long gray hair snaking down her back in a pair of braids, to her heavy denim skirt, to her jangly earrings and necklace and bracelets that rattled as she stirred and stirred. Whether she was being demure or coy or just annoying, she knew something, he could tell. But he didn't know how to respond, didn't want to risk getting thrown out. "Can you tell me if he's here, and if I can go see him? Just point the way and I'll find it, I'm sure."

"You don't know who you are, do you?" the woman asked, her eyes on Blake as her hand kept moving slowly above the pot.

"Excuse me?"

"When a man doesn't know who he really is, he can never know if he is truly good or bad." She stepped back from the pot and set down the spoon. Blake looked at her, then took in the room, the galley kitchen, the old stove that looked like it had been forged in cast iron, the gas-powered burners with various pots, the long pine table and nearly 20 chairs surrounding it, the large, carpeted space to his right that appeared to be some kind of play area or school for toddlers. A hallway jutted from a door to the back of the kitchen, leading to an unknown number of rooms that held an unknown number of people. "Those are the words of our leader, our founder, and you should heed them. All men should."

"Yeah, sure." The air seemed muggier, heavier than when he'd walked in, maybe it was the strange concoction brewing that seemed to emit some kind of essence of oil. He held his ground, roped up by an unseen lasso, ready to burst outside into the cold but unwilling to give up on finding out about Lena. "I can't disagree with that. Is your leader here? Maybe I can talk to him instead of Eric."

"No, you may see Eric. If you walk hard enough and long enough you will reach him. He visits the temple every day at this time. Take the path, stay firm, do not stray, and you can have your conversation." She smiled at him then, and it seemed so kind, so genuine, that Blake instinctively smiled back. A door opened, somewhere down the long hall, and the woman turned back to her task, removed the pot from the heat, covered it with a moist white towel, and retreated into the darkness of the rear of the building.

He walked out into the apathetic chill, the crushing emptiness of the place slowly giving way, he could see, to some kind of activity. A pair of women, long denim skirts hanging beneath big black coats and swishing against the snow, carried white canvas sacks in each arm toward the entrance Blake had just come out of. Their eyes, pale blue and lively, stayed on him as they pushed inside and closed the door sharply behind them. Laughter, children's laughter, floated from beyond a small hill, and he could hear a large, rumbling engine clattering far away. The path, he realized, did not delve into the community, toward the wisps of smoke rising from nearby houses, but instead pushed slightly up and away, into the dense, old-growth forest spreading long and deep in the distance. He followed it.

"Do you know how many rituals and practices are in place to ensure purity and cleanliness in religions throughout the world? In Islam, for example, there is the salah, the daily, standardized prayer practiced five times per day, which requires a basic level of washing and cleansing before it can be performed. There is also a full ablution that needs to take place after certain physical acts and before certain rituals and prayers. There are strict dietary laws, and there are specific focuses on grooming, sexual, and bathroom etiquette. The Hindus must pay homage to their ancestors in the Ganges River and cleanse themselves of sin in its waters. Indigenous peoples here in the Americas performed ceremonies in conjunction with purifying rituals conducted in sweat lodges. Judaism and Christianity have untold numbers of laws and practices for any and all situations that have been performed throughout the centuries, and of course Baptism is, for us and many others, the ultimate in ritual purification.

"I tell you all of this, Eric, because we are required, now, to perform our own ritual. In order for her to properly return to us, to become a true Chronicler once again and to continue our mission, she must also be purified. It must be done soon, and she must be cleansed with natural, untampered water. And you must be the one to compel her to this action."

"How? I don't have your power, your vision, your abilities. I can try, I will, but I need something more."

"Your questions must stop. Now. You will have what you need, you will lift a veil and she will see my face. She'll listen to you, as she has listened to me, and you will say the words and perform the rituals that are necessary in order to bring her back into the fold."

"The rituals?"

"Yes. There is another trial that you must perform."

Chapter 25

The light trotted away from Blake, skipped through the bald tree trunks and limbs and branches and bathed the woods in the heaviest light he'd ever seen. He crunched through, stepping on packed snow and wet twigs and compacted leaves, ignoring the cold in his legs, the thudding in his head, the weight of a boulder on his chest. Lena had to be around, had to be in Bochim, in some shack, in the temple, but he couldn't do anything but walk and try to prepare himself for whatever strangeness he was set to encounter.

The path ascended, descended, curved, straightened, he couldn't keep track of the geography or the topography, he couldn't ascertain north from south, but he kept moving through the light, hoping the temple was nearby and he could put an end to everything.

A squawk from above, a crow, a black bird, he looked up and spotted its darkness in the highest tree, at the peak of a towering oak, eyeing him, eyeing its surroundings, glowering at everything. Another sound reverberated, and he snapped his attention back to the path ahead. It seemed to both narrow and widen, the trees grew thinner and the snow seemed to loosen and give way to larger rocks that poked harshly at the soles of his feet. Up ahead, a bridge, made by hand, he thought, the span seemed to disappear into the craggy embankment without proper support, there were no railings or arches, and a rush of water had, in the not too distant past, knocked loose some of the heavy gray stones piled on either side of the dry creek bed.

He didn't know what to expect, the word temple evoked some pretty fantastical thoughts, monumental structures and awe-inspiring designs and ancient, magisterial sights, but instead he encountered something basic. Something simple and almost suburban in its construction and execution. As he crossed over the creek and the bridge, he saw the temple a couple of dozen yards away. A plain, square building, perhaps two stories high, hovered in the near-distance, the lower portion resplendent with the kind of bright limestone found throughout central Indiana. It only reached 7 feet high, though, before it shifted to wood siding painted light gray, and fascia painted white, that connected with a roof pitched at a flat, unnatural depth. It seemed so normal, so boring, even the columns, clad in stucco, jutting from the stone into the roof, looked phony and did not fit in with the surroundings. There was no cross, no sign or indication of what the place was called, no special landscaping, just more gravel leading from the bridge to the entrance.

The inside of his mouth had dried up, and he slid his hand into the sliver of pocket tucked into the torso of his coat, retrieved the little bottle, downed the rest of the whiskey. He stood by the large mahogany door and decided against knocking, shoved the empty bottle back into its spot and pushed the burnished bronze handle down and walked in slowly, navigated the turns, and carefully entered the sanctuary. Wood paneling screamed at him from every angle, he'd expected something more grand, more ornate, but the interior reminded him of a cheap lodge he'd seen once on a ski trip to northern Indiana. He also expected soaring ceilings, arches, marble, gold, spires, art, ambience, anything to indicate Bochim's temple was a special place. Instead, he saw folding chairs from a VFW hall, battery-powered candles from Big Lots, scuffed laminate floors, a stage built less than two feet high and decorated with plastic greenery resting on mismatched end tables.

But a man sat on the stage, swallowed by a massive wooden chair, a desiccated, gray-haired, gray-bearded, hunkered man in black slacks, a black overcoat, and black boots. He appeared to be sleeping, his head had slumped onto his right shoulder and his chest rose and fell in a solemn pattern.

"May I help you?" said a voice that seemed to slip out of the man.

"Um, yeah. Hi. My name is Blake, and I'm looking for a guy named Eric."

"Yes, Eric, many people are looking for him," the voice said again, and Blake could not see whether or not the man's mouth had even opened. "You seek him for what purpose?"

"I'm writing a story, I'm a freelance writer and I wanted to talk about your community, and I was told Eric could provide me with a lot of good information." Blake waited for a response, but fatigue seemed to have overtaken the old man once again, and his head lolled and bobbed silently. Blake moved closer, tapped the arm of the chair, but got no response, and looked around again. At first glance the room, just as large and just as unassuming as a Kingdom Hall sanctuary, seemed to have only one way in and out, the mahogany door he'd walked through, with no restrooms or storage areas or electrical closets. He stepped on the stage, felt the creak of the wood under his feet, moved slowly to the back wall, ran his hand along the fake wood and came to a heavy crease, two strips of paneling came together awkwardly and he realized there was some kind of seal that could be opened, and he pushed into the wall and felt it swing open.

Darkness. Blackness. Nothingness. Not even the faint lights of the sanctuary could penetrate the emptiness. He leaned in, squinted into the dark, and felt a hand clamp around his throat.

"Please, don't move, for your own sake," a separate, unfamiliar voice echoed from somewhere in the depths of the room. "He's so much stronger than you can imagine."

Blake didn't flinch, and could barely breathe, let alone form or utter a word. The grip tightened slightly, and it pushed him back into the sanctuary. That face, that hair. The giant from the woods stared down at him, his eyes screaming with hatred, and Blake stared back while trying not to gasp or cough or let a stray tear slip through.

"You're looking for me, I suppose," the voice offered, and Blake tried to nod but couldn't dip his head an inch. "Eric Hagedorn, second patriarchate of the Church of Reformation of Bochim. Nice to meet you, Mr. Prince."

The grip loosened enough for Blake to speak, and he took in a handful of shallow breaths before asking, "What? How do you know me?"

"You don't need to know that, but here I am. You have questions for me?"

"Um, yeah. Can you ask this guy to let me go?"

"Yes, I can do that. He listens to us, and I hope you will, too."

"OK, I will." A nod from Eric and the hand released from Blake's neck, but the hulking figure remained, the grip around his arm instead of his neck. The old man in the chair hadn't moved, or made a sound. The lights in the sanctuary flickered, the wind whipped outside and cold slivers of air slipped through the seams of the building. "I just wanted to talk, to ask you about your community up here. I write, you know, for a magazine, and I have my own blog."

"Yes, I'm aware of what you do, and why you're here. Looking for information about us, looking for cracks in the walls of our utopia. I understand, but you're not the first."

"No, it's not about that. I'm a writer, I'm just here to tell a story."

"Do not meddle in what you do not understand," the old man whispered, and Blake turned to look at him, his head still tilted down, his body undisturbed and still. "We know how people live their lives, and it is damaging, unproductive, and sinful. We are here to fix that."

"How?"

"Any way we can. With anyone and with anything that will help us achieve that."

"I mean, honestly, that just sounds kind of crazy, " Blake said, and immediately regretted his strong word choice.

"Me, us, we're the opposite of crazy. We are Godly, and you are all masquerading as human beings every day, every minute." The old man finally stirred, looked up at Blake and eyed him carefully, then dropped his head back down. "Joseph, have you searched him yet?"

The hand tightened around Blake's biceps, and another hand felt around his pants pockets, the front and the back, pulled out his cell phone and car keys, dropped them to the stage in a clattering mess. Joseph, the mythically strong behemoth fumbling around Blake's torso, breathed heavily, his eyes darting wildly around the heavy black parka and maroon hoodie, until his fingers felt the sliver of wood and metal in the breast pocket of the coat, stuffed between a wad of tissue Blake had yanked from his cup holder. The knife seemed tiny in the monstrous, gnarled white hand, and he handed it to Eric solemnly and squeezed Blake's arm even tighter.

"You know, I've met people before who wanted to harm me, who hated me so bad I could smell it coming out of them. And honestly, I appreciated it. More so than this silly reporter's ruse you've come up with," Eric said. "Evil and hatred have built up in you, and I can see that you're just bursting with devilish words for me."

"I can't explain any of this, any of you," Blake said quietly. "All I hate is that three little kids are gone, that Jessie, an innocent woman, is gone. And for what? For who?"

Something stirred in the old man, a fit of air lodged in his chest that fought its way out in a heaving, hacking crackle of sound. "Do you know what my daughter believed? Do you know the opposite of faith?" He lifted his head again, stared at Blake with thin, watery eyes, and coughed into his fist for several seconds. "It is doubt, unbelief, denial. And we cannot permit that to fester here."

"You're talking about your own daughter," Blake yelled. "She died. And her kids, your grandkids. They're gone, they all died, goddamnit."

"She was not clean, she was not pure, she could not travel from darkness to light, her deviance could not be transmitted into morality," the old man said calmly, like he was explaining why a gift certificate was no longer valid. "The children were a piece of her, a part of her sin, I cannot mourn what was absent and inferior."

"And so you killed them all? You proved, once and for all, how rigid and tyrannical and insane you all really are."

The hand squeezed around his arm tighter, and Blake winced in pain and bent over. "She failed, young man, she had gone aside, was defiled, and strayed. She made an oath to us long ago, to me, to her brothers, to the church and the community, and abandoned it all. I gave her a chance to return to us, and she did not pass the ordeal set forth by God and administered by Eric."

"What ordeal? What are you-"

"I am the first patriarchate of Bochim, of the Church of Reformation. I speak for God!" the old man bellowed, rising out of his seat a foot or so before slamming back down onto the wood. "We are living in utopia, in our own heaven, right here in Bochim, wallowing in its joy every single day, no matter how the outside world views us. We are living a wonderful privilege, and my daughter could not see that, and had to endure the judgement of God."

The echoes of his voice faded in the temple, and Blake looked around in befuddlement. These people, he thought, will stop at nothing to glorify their own beliefs, to lift their patronizing nightmare of theology into a doctrine of terror that could consume anyone they wanted. The massive beast holding his arm, Joseph, glowered down at him with an expression of pious anger, ready to damage Blake as soon as he received the word.

"Well, yeah, I can't argue with any of that. But you know, people can disbelieve and doubt anything, even what they see with their own eyes," Blake offered, ready to accept the punishment doled out by the behemoth and the old man.

"What is there to doubt?" Eric asked from behind the old man, whose name Blake had not heard anyone in the community utter since he'd arrived.

He felt his whole life was being condensed into a few minutes, the unbending moments in front of him so brittle and fragile and ready to snap at any second unless he found a way to steel himself to an unknown task. "You, this, everything you stand for. You're not right, what you're saying and doing is just a code for evil, perpetrated by this old bastard, because whatever life did to him was enough to send him here to pollute you all with this fire-and-brimstone nonsense that ends up with a woman and her kids dead in the snow. That ends up with poor black girls in Louisville killed. That ends up with an innocent woman disappeared. By you."

No one said a word, the only sounds were the old man's breathing and the wind whistling against the roof and seeping through cracks in the stones. Eric shifted on his feet and rubbed his hands together, avoided looking at Blake, but the old man stared hard through muted gray eyes, processing something Blake couldn't understand.

"Where's Lena? What'd you do with her?" Blake finally asked, looking at Eric but speaking to all, including Joseph, who hadn't uttered a word but seemed steadfast in his devotion to intimidation and pain.

"I don't know anything about her," Eric said sullenly, almost like he wished he had an answer.

"We have no use for those who aren't adherents, she is no one to me and has never been inside the boundaries of our community," the old man said.

"Eric, what'd you do to her? Come on, man, not another woman, not this one, too."

"It's not-" Eric started, and looked down at the wooden floor, shuffled back to the small bench off the stage and sat down. "She's not here. I tried, I talked to her, but she wouldn't listen. I gave her a chance. She wouldn't listen."

"What?" Blake growled, and felt the heat simmering inside his chest, rising to his face and his head. A whisper of cool, fresh air brushed his forehead. He squeezed his muscles and lunged toward Eric, the powerful grasp tightened even further and he struggled to get free, started to slump to the ground and breathe heavier and harder. "What'd you do? Where-"

The hands shot to his body and lifted him in the air, and Blake's sense of equilibrium shifted and slanted as he got tossed like a sandbag against the rear wall of the temple and crashed into the stone and wood in a sloppy heap. He groaned and reached for his lower back, amazed that his hefty coat hadn't softened the blow any. "Poor black girls? Lena? You talk like you know us and our methods and our theology," the old man said. "We have proved the superiority of our devotion in so many ways, and we are not put out by death. We are not permitted to fail, and Eric and Joseph have succeeded in all the ways you have not."

A heavy boot pressed into Blake's sternum, and he gasped and gulped and coughed. "So you told Eric to kill those black women in Louisville. That's how you do things, that's how God talks to you?"

"We did what?" Briefly, the old man dropped his pretensions and squinted hard at Blake, like he was trying to figure out the intentions in Blake's comment. "I don't know about any black whores or anything you're talking about."

"Tell him, Eric," Blake rasped.

Eric sputtered and folded his arms and rocked back and forth on his feet like a toddler, unable to open his mouth and speak what Blake had decided had to be true.

"Tell him you've been going after girls, that you took care of Jessie and decided there were others that had to be put out of the way, that had to be terrified by you. And you latched on to me and came after me and used me to fulfill the wishes of this old man. And now-"

The boot pressed harder, and Blake could no longer talk, could barely breathe, and put his palms against the sole and tried to push Joseph off, didn't even get the foot an inch off his chest, and squirmed and heaved as hard as he could, to no avail. The air grew colder. Breaths quickened, shortened, became shallow, high-pitched gasps, chest numbed, arms numbed, head numbed. He closed his eyes and squeezed every muscle in his body.

A sound rushed into his ears, he thought at first it was nothing but the air shimmying into the seams of the temple, his own choked breathing that he had trouble hearing. But he recognized it, finally, a slight shuffling, rubber on stone, a pair of shoes. Then another sound, like the whir of a fly passing by an ear, and Blake turned his head in time to see a blur of motion pass across his line of sight, and heard a thud connect just above him, and the pressure released from his chest and he gasped as hard and fast as he could.

"Blake!" a voice shouted. Tyner. "Get up, man!" He was there. Blake rolled over and looked up to see Tyner wielding a long, crooked tree branch, and he slammed it into Joseph's arm, then his stomach, then his arm again, the wood shattering and showering the floor in thin splinters. A succession of blows followed, the wood crunching into Joseph's face, spraying blood into the wall, and Blake scrambled to his feet to face Eric.

"Get him, you coward," the old man grunted at Eric. "Don't be like your father, that quitter, that nothing. Do something!" Eric stood still for a moment, absorbing the insults, then rushed forward in a flurry of spastic, spindly arms. Blake stepped aside and launched a right hook, connected with the cheek and the jaw in a solid punch, and Eric yelped and stopped moving to cradle his face in his hands. Blake felt around in his jacket, grabbed a hold of the bottle, and pulled it out.

"You brought her here, you've got Lena," Blake grunted, Eric shook his head, still cradling his face, and didn't say anything, as Tyner and Joseph scuffled in the background. "You killed those girls, killed 'em for no reason. And whatever you did to Jessie and those kids-" Blake's voice caught, and he stepped forward and braced his lower half, and delivered a kick to Eric's midsection that dropped him to the ground. Behind them, Blake could see Joseph had ripped away the branch and thrown it aside and pushed his hands against Tyner's throat, trying to wrap his powerful fingers around the bare skin. Blake skipped forward with the bottle and smashed it into the back of Joseph's head with a sickening crack. The bottle refused to shatter but Joseph buckled, his scalp opened up and began to bleed profusely, and Tyner pushed him to the ground and threw a handful of sharp punches.

A gurgling cough interrupted the fighting, and Blake dropped the bottle and turned to see the old man trying to rise to his feet, walked over and shoved him back into the big wooden seat. "You've ruined your utopia, Bezalel. You came here for love and you've ended it with hate." Something stirred, Blake turned and saw Eric on the ground, cradling the small knife Joseph had taken out of Blake's pocket. Blake faced Eric, squared himself and prepared to fend off the attack, but Eric rushed past him to Bezalel with the curved blade and raked it across the old man's throat. Bright red liquid trickled down into the gray, peppery beard, and Eric dropped the knife onto the floor.

Tyner pulled at Blake, Joseph had crumpled to the floor, blood spattered and drenching his clothes, his face, his shoes. "Come on, B." He tugged again, and Blake started for the front before turning and seeing Tyner at the little seam in the back wall. They entered the small back room, the only light a yellow glow coming from a dangling bulb that barely illuminated the concrete floors and walls. Blake saw a couple of tables scattered with papers and books, a line of shelves packed with more books, including a massive Bible embroidered with gold lettering, some black robes hanging from tall hooks, unlit candles, cardboard boxes shoved along the back wall. Tyner kicked aside one of the boxes and dropped to his backside and slid forward. "Let's go," he huffed, and disappeared.

Blake started for the wall but stopped, slipped back to the sanctuary opening and crouched down, looking for movement from anyone inside. Nothing, the old man had slumped halfway off his chair, Joseph remained on the ground by the back wall, and Eric had disappeared. Blake rushed in, grabbed the bottle, smeared with blood, off the floor and shoved it into his pocket, along with his keys and phone. The knife was nowhere to be seen. He ran back into the room and slid down into the hidden opening, dropped down five feet or so into a deeper, danker room. Cut out of the earth and lined with limestone and creek stone, the room forced both guys to duck down to accommodate the low ceiling, the width so meager they could stretch their arms and touch the sides of the walls easily. Newspaper clippings, pages from the Bible, articles and pictures printed from the Internet, small tables dotted with bottles and vials, and photos of Jessie, young and fresh-faced and beautiful and dressed in a long skirt and white blouse, were taped to the walls, but Blake didn't have time to stop and look at any of it before seeing Tyner motioning to him from the end of the room, where the floor tilted down and led to another passage. Before he went in, though, he glanced at one of the photos of Jessie, her age somewhat indeterminate but she might have been around 13 or 14 years old. And she was wearing a small necklace with a cross.

They crouched down and crawled through a tunnel, their heads scraping the rock and clay above them, their knees and hands dragging against the sandstone slabs laid below, with the screen from Tyner's cell phone providing enough light for them to just make out the way ahead. Blake lost track of their time in the tunnel, could have been 15 minutes or 50 minutes, Tyner didn't say a word as he pressed forward and Blake never asked what time it was or where they were headed. The passage started to ramp up, and Tyner set his phone on the ground, propped himself on his knees and pressed his hands into the ceiling. A creak and a groan, and a little door popped open, letting in shafts of pure white light. Tyner lifted himself out into the deadening cold, and Blake followed, not surprised to find himself in a barren patch of trees that looked like any snatch of woods that could be found anywhere in Hudson County. They slammed the lid closed and ran off as quietly as they could, their feet swishing through piles of snow and their bodies brushing past branches and limbs and thorny bushes. Blake looked back, unsure how Tyner had been able to find the little entrance without a sign or marker that was visible, and nearly crashed into the back of his friend.

"Gotta climb through here," Tyner said, and bent down to go through a small opening in a wire fence. Tufts of black hair were stuck to little barbs here and there, and Blake scanned for signs of a herd of some kind, then ducked down and slipped through the opening and took off behind Tyner as they ran parallel to the fence line for a few minutes, traipsing through the footprints left earlier. Across the pasture, an old farmhouse seemed ready to implode on itself, the only thing supporting the boards and framing was a foundation of hand-hewn creek stones stacked six-feet high. A gray shed stood ahead of the two guys, the aluminum roof rusted and the siding curled out at the bottom, some rotting, crumbling pallets leaned against the front, an ancient plow poked its tines and handles out of the snow, and Tyner's car sat nearby, just a few feet from the road curving around a bend. They climbed in and sped away, Blake not even sure how to lead them back to where his car was parked until he spotted a road sign that proclaimed, "Welcome to Hudson County," and they swerved and skidded and slowed to take a turn onto a state road that took them past the entrance to Bochim and, finally, found Blake's car.

"Thanks," Blake said quietly, not even sure how much to say, how to communicate about what they'd just seen and done. "You going home?"

"Yeah, in a bit. Gotta stop and see momma first, check in on her. You know."

"I know." Blake opened the car door, let the cold sweep inside for a moment before putting a foot out onto the snow. "Alright then, T." He reached over, dapped him up, and got out of the car.

"Hit me up sometime, B."

"Yeah, I will," he said, closed the door, and watched Tyner pull onto the road and drive down into Troy City. He got into his Camry, cranked the engine and sat with the blowers on full blast for a couple of minutes, sitting and staring. Pulled away, finally, drove slowly, his hands not shaking but not entirely steady, his eyes scanning everything in sight as the car rumbled along in silence. He grabbed for his phone in one of the dense jacket pockets, plugged in the auxiliary cord, and scrolled through his Rolodex of a couple of thousand songs with this thumbs, hoping to find something that would make him feel better, eventually settled on the shuffle button and was relieved to hear the delicate, introspective sounds of an acoustic piano, then the masterful Moog bass, played with impeccable timing and unmatched soul, and the soft drums, and the acoustic guitar, and then the voice of Stevie singing, "Looking in your eyes, kind of heaven eyes." She wasn't there, she was just gone, and Blake had to wonder if he had something to do with it.

The car followed Tyner's tire marks, and Blake looked over at the spot in the woods, the hanging geodes, and wondered if things in Bochin would change. And saw a face, a blonde, square head, and an exceedingly tall, wiry frame pressed against the trees. Then it disappeared, and he drove away as fast as the roads would allow.

Chapter 26

Blake stood next to the hospital bed, his hands gripping the hard plastic railing while he tried not to stare at Amos' damaged face and head. Gauze and tape were wrapped around his shaved skull, and spots of blood had seeped through the bandaging near his temple. Dark bruises crept from beneath his eyes, and a large bandage covered his nose, while tubes crept out of his nostrils and a collar held his neck in place. But he was awake, his eyes big and responsive, and he kept his gaze level and steady.

"Got a little crazy up there," Blake said, not even sure what he could reveal to Amos, still a cop, still capable of reaching out to the right people and causing trouble for Tyner and Blake. "Don't know what Landa said. But we didn't really find anything, not Lena, not anything related to what happened to you. But man, they're not right, none of them."

Amos gave a little eye roll, he probably had dealt with some of the people up there through his years in the state police. The monitors and machines beeped, the equipment blinked, and the TV mounted high in the corner raced silently through basketball and hockey highlights. Landa had been in earlier but left to get food, and Blake rocked a little from foot to foot, wondering how much time he had. Things were cool with them, she'd apologized and forgiven him, in her way, for what happened to Amos, but he still had trouble being straight with her. Always had.

"Eric met with Jessie, spoke to her, tried to convince her of her rightful place in Bochim and all kinds of nonsense, but I don't know exactly what happened, or how. Doesn't matter, the old man in charge of the place was behind it, he hated her because she left him and left their life, and wanted to force her to go back, but whatever they did to her or asked her to do made her die out there in the snow, and the kids, too.

"There was all kinds of stuff in that temple, pictures, books, weird liquids and tinctures, so much I didn't even get a chance to see. I think they gave her some kind of homemade potion, that's why the tox report came back with such strange results. And they were keeping track of people, keeping an eye on me, us, Lena, other women. They follow such bizarre rituals and rules and beliefs that don't correspond to how any church I know operates. Control, and penance, and oaths, and ordeals, they're, like, from another century. But I got outta there, safely, and you all know what to look for now, I hope."

A vibration, the phone, and Blake looked at it to see a message from his mom. He went and opened the door and looked around the halls for Landa, returned to the bedside and shoved his phone back into his pocket. The door opened and a nurse entered, nearly startled Blake with her swell of curly hair and overdone makeup and syrupy accent that didn't seem to belong to Troy or Hudson, but he'd been there long enough to know you could always find someone with a southern twang even though they were hundreds of miles from the real south. She did her thing, checked vitals and bandages and pushed buttons and pecked at a computer tethered to a slew of other equipment, smiled sweetly at Blake, almost seductively, and left them alone again.

A crumple of sound tried to escape Amos' lips, and Blake leaned forward, trying to hear him, and Amos coughed hard and opened his lips. "They fffffound 'em," he said in a nasty rasp.

"Found who?" Blake asked nervously, knowing the answer but not wanting to give anything away, not even to Amos.

"The old mmmmmmman. And the guy. In the temple. Both with sssssslit thhhhhroats."

"What guy?"

"The gggggggguy. The little guy." Blake stared, Amos' eyes had retreated a little but remained steadfast on his brother-in-law. He knew nothing about it, nothing about what Tyner and Blake had seen or done, but he knew something serious. He knew Eric was dead.

"Big brother!" A ruckus of vocals and plastic bags and feet interrupted and Blake saw Landa coming into the room, her hands full and her face beaming with energy. "You want something to eat? I got a bunch of chicken sandwiches, some fries, no drinks, though, I hate carrying drinks, I hate the little cardboard carrier they give you, it's so awkward. Ame, you OK? Did the nurse come in, she was supposed to be back, I asked her before I left. No pickles, right, boo?" Landa snatched one of the sandwiches from a bag and unwrapped it, peeled off two puny green slices and tossed them back in the bag, placed two brown napkins under the sandwich and brought it slowly to Amos' chest.

"You alright, sis? Have you gotten any sleep, has mom or anyone given you a break?"

"I'm fine, slept over there on that mini-couch, I'm great now."

"OK. Well, I guess I'll head home, mom's been checking in with me for a while." He started to reach for Amos but stopped, tapped him on the foot, patted Landa's shoulder, and grabbed one of the sandwiches and gave a little wave before pushing himself into the hall. The elevator went down, slow and cranky, and Blake devoured the sandwich and tossed the wrapper in a garbage can before he left the hospital lobby. He got in his car and left the parking lot with no intention of going home, not right away, and found himself steering toward the liquor store down the road, the shop squished between a little church and a tattoo parlor in a depressing looking strip mall that had once caught fire and nearly burned to the ground. Inside, he stared at the bottles, at the brownest bourbons, at the big, heavy, 750-ml. monstrosities he'd bought so many times. But he walked away, went to the clerk, pointed behind her head and asked for a pint of Knob Creek. Almost the same price as the cheap stuff, less whiskey, sure, but higher quality, so maybe it's worth it, he thought, maybe it means something.

The streets of Troy City looked clean, swept free of snow and ice, though Blake could see crystals of salt on the asphalt. Who's gonna speak for the black girls, he thought as he listened to the plaintive tenor saxes crying out for Lester Young in Mingus' classic tune. Maybe there'd be some activists in Louisville, true leaders and believers who could fight and scream and get the word out, who knew that the lives of those women, those downtrodden and disenfranchised and broken and beautiful and hard headed girls, hadn't ended for nothing.

Try as he might, though, he couldn't stop thinking about Jessie and the kids, couldn't let go of a guilt and anger he wasn't sure he could understand. He didn't have to feel bad anymore, but there was nothing else to replace the thoughts of so much death. There was his music, his movies, his shows, his writing, but as he pulled into the spot by his apartment and looked up at his parents' house, he realized that was all he had.

He watched her pull to a stop, the van cranking out voluminous gusts of exhaust as it idled on the snow-covered gravel. The fictions of the world poured onto him, the thoughts and ideals that had been drilled into his life were wrong, God was not humble, simple, compassionate, God drained everything out of him and was an unyielding, uncaring force every single day. But he obeyed, he always did, he had to.

She got out on her own and looked around, the environs of St. Aureus and its surroundings still unfamiliar to her, even though she'd gone walking with the kids around parts of the campus during the fall. The headlights of the van kept him away, as did the thought of confronting her in the darkness, alone, when he had no business being there without Bezalel. But he stepped forward through the snow, being careful not to crunch any sticks and alert her, and clutched the little bottle in his gloved hand. Every part of his body shook, and when she went back to the van and lifted out the baby and tugged on the puffy arms of the two small kids, he reached out for a tree and held on for a minute, nearly letting go of his previous meal in the snow, but he breathed in deeply for a few seconds and felt it pass.

"Bilhah," Eric said into the darkness, not too loud, not too soft, enough for her to turn and stare at the space where her old name had emerged from. "It's OK, it's me, Eric. Don't be afraid, I don't want to hurt you or anything."

"What's going on? Where's my father?"

"He isn't well, he asked me to come instead."

"Oh. Well, can we go somewhere else? It's freezing, and, like, pitch-black out."

"Yeah, we can go. But there's something we need to do first."

"OK." Eric waved at the kids and smiled, reaching into his pocket and holding out a small cross dangling from a delicate gold chain.

Epilogue

Blake walked slowly down the stairs holding the Pyrex dish, his hand covered in an overstuffed oven mitt, and walked slowly across the slippery concrete to the back door. He knocked and opened the door in one motion, wiping his wet shoes on the mat. Most of the snowfall from the past month had melted into endless cascades of clear water falling from trees and eaves and gutters and car ports that became solemn, gray puddles of mush.

"Hey," he said as he stepped into the kitchen, and set the dish on the kitchen counter. "Still hot, let's eat soon."

"Sure, the bread's almost done and Landa's salad is ready." Mariana smiled and pulled out a quartet of white plates rimmed with blue scrollwork, her favorite set of dishes she'd brought from Germany, while Landa filled glasses with ice water and took a red plastic bowl of hearty greens and carrots and nuts and blue cheese. Amos sat alone at the table, hands folded across his stomach, his eyes watching the proceedings but his body totally still. Most of his faculties had returned after the brain injury but he couldn't do much physically, walked with a cane, wrote and typed slowly, relied on Landa for rides to work and back, and had been relegated to desk work at an auxiliary office staffed with state cops. But he maintained the same calm demeanor, never blamed Blake for what happened, and displayed no anger toward the denizens of Bochim.

"Landa, you back to work full-time yet?" Blake asked as the four sat around the table a few minutes later, digging into the baked ziti he'd made in his apartment.

"No, another couple of weeks, I think. My boss has been cool," she said in between mouthfuls of lettuce and baked bread. "What about you, you going back to the warehouse at all?"

"No, no, never, that was so boring and stupid, it's not even worth the little paycheck that I got. I'll stick with writing, I'm getting more assignments and jobs, so it's going OK."

"What about medical school, you can go back, right? Start up again in your, what, second semester?"

"I could, yeah, they have a rule," Blake said, and swiped the last bite of pasta from his plate. "But, I don't know, that's just not me, I don't think. That was dad. That was him."

The table remained quiet, other than the clink of forks on porcelain. Mariana sipped her glass of red wine, the only alcohol on the table, and looked at her kids. Blake had predicted he would be gently evicted from the apartment, at some point, after a string of tense conversations he'd had with his mom, but she backed off after Amos was injured, and seemed to accept Blake's flaws and attributes. He was not a great son, he knew that, but he'd vowed to be better.

"Maybe you cccccccan write something about that place," Amos said. "Contact the ppppppppaper here and talk about everything."

"Yeah, that's a good idea." The dinner wound down, Blake had let go of DJ duties and kept quiet while his mom played Journey and Hall & Oates and Howard Jones tracks on a loop, and the three of them cleaned and packed up the leftovers while Amos slowly used the bathroom and ambled to the mudroom to fetch his jacket and put on his shoes.

"You talked to Tyner recently? Is he doing OK?" Landa asked as she put on a long purple coat.

"He's good, he actually took a leave from work and went to Florida, he's working with a private trainer to get back in shape and try out for some pro teams."

"Oh, good for him." They doled out hugs and handshakes and left, leaving Blake alone with his mom.

"How have you been sleeping? Do you need some melatonin? I have CBD oil, too," Mariana said.

"No, I've been good the last few days, thanks, though."

"Your father always said the two of you were sand and water, did you know that?" she asked, and Blake shook his head at the invocation of his dad. "And he said water washes away sand, so he was careful not to push you too hard, at times. He didn't want you to suffer because of his beliefs and expectations of what you should be."

"Oh."

"But, you know, water and sand can also create beautiful things. Don't suffer and settle for all this because you're afraid of destroying something. Create a new life, do what you want, but use your imagination and your heart, please." She reached out and hugged him, finally, squeezing with a purity he hadn't felt from her in a long time.

"Alright, thanks. Love you."

He sat on the couch, not even sure how much time had passed as he cruised around the Internet, his work finished and turned in, his mind wandering between heavier thoughts and simpler pursuits, scrolling through videos of obscure R&B and soul artists from the 70s and 80s, talented musicians with minimal followings and meager Wikipedia pages. Nothing seemed different, he wasn't overjoyed with life, but he felt better, stronger even, as what he'd witnessed had forced him to think more freely about how he moved through his day-to-day.

But he was alone, again. Lena had returned to work, he'd been told that she'd showed up for her regular shift just a few days after Blake and Tyner went to Bochim. She'd kept her distance, though, didn't text or call to let him know of her whereabouts, leaving him in an odd state of simply wanting to hear from her and see her, but not wanting to mess with her life, not if she wasn't feeling him anymore. He'd never projected any kind of feelings toward another person the way he had with her, and he wished she could see that, no matter what had happened to him, no matter what he'd been through, he trusted her to deal with his past and not use anything to hurt him.

For about the hundredth time in the past week or so, he thought about getting in his car and driving over to her place, driving to the hospital, just to see her and ensure that she was handling things, but he slid further onto the couch and tried to find something mindless to watch. He settled on a basketball game, a cutthroat contest between bitter rivals that meant absolutely nothing to him, and went into the kitchen to find something to eat. There was some of the leftover pasta from dinner with his mom and sister, some cold rice he could stir-fry with frozen edamame, carrots, and soy sauce, or he could order a medium pepperoni-and-mushroom from Rafael's Pizza downtown and pick it up in half an hour.

On the counter, by his car keys, he spotted a takeout menu. Tariq's. The smells of the restaurant hit him, the spices and the grill, as well as the image of Lena sitting in the booth, the twinkle in her eyes, the depth of her voice, and he picked it up and smiled. A knock from the outside door echoed, and Blake went downstairs and opened the door slowly with the menu still in his grasp.

"Hey." Lena stood a few feet away, her feet scraping delicately against the mushy ice on the walkway, her body enmeshed in a puffy blue coat and black pants.

"Hi. Are you- how are you?" Blake said and stepped out into the cold in his shorts and t-shirt.

"I'm good, I'm good. You?"

"Yeah, you know, doing alright." They stared at each other, their hands stuffed into pockets, their mouths shooting out puffs of white breath. A car rushed by, a plane roared overhead, a dog barked in a nearby yard. The sounds of Troy City, Blake thought, and he and Lena continued to stand and smile blandly on the sidewalk. "I guess you're doing OK, huh? Back to work and everything."

"I'm sorry, Blake. I know I should have talked to you or gotten back to you, but when I realized what was going on, when I knew someone was watching me, I just left." She stepped forward, like she wanted to reach out to Blake, but stopped and wrapped her arms around her waist. "I wanted to call you, but with everything going on and all the craziness happening, I decided to take my vacation time for a little break, and not let anyone know."

"I get it. I understand," Blake said, and remained by the door in his lightweight clothing, rocking back and forth and rubbing his forearms. "I'm just glad you're safe. I was worried."

"I was afraid of them, I really was," she said with true fear in her voice. "There were messages on my phone, then I started getting paranoid every time I saw a car following me or parked outside. I wanted to stay off the radar for a little while, so I went to Waukesha to stay with my parents. And it's not that I didn't trust you or wanted you to worry, but those people-" she trailed off and looked down at the ground.

"It's alright," he said, and tried to reach her eyes with his own. "You're here, I'm here."

"You know, when I was married before, it took me a long time to realize what was happening, to accept that what I was doing was helping to drive him deeper into the cycle of addiction, and that I was just enabling it all.

"And you didn't do anything, not like he did, and I didn't act the same way I did with him, but I realized I had to leave, just like I did with him. Not because of you, but because it was the right thing for me to do."

Blake took his toe and kicked aside some loose, chunky snow from the sidewalk, looked up at Lena, her head covered in a white beanie, strands of red hair falling out seductively in the back and on the sides. Without thinking, he moved to her and offered his arms, and she accepted the hug, buried her head in his shoulder and stood with him in the shadow of the garage.

"So, do you want to come in?" he asked as they pulled away from the lengthy embrace.

She shook her head and put her hands back in her pockets. "No, thanks. I really just wanted to stop by and let you know what I've been up to and that I'm alright."

"Maybe we can grab something to eat somewhere."

Another shake, a step back. "I just need to focus on other things right now, my life at the hospital, my career, on helping people."

"Oh." So it goes, he thought, the end of our thing. "Well, I'd like to call you sometime, just to see how you're doing in a few days or whatever."

"I don't know," she said, taking another step back, toward the street. "We'll see each other, I'm sure. Maybe soon." A wave, and a smile, and she turned around and walked to her Volkswagen parked on the slushy, salty street.

He waved back, and watched her drive off, then went back inside the garage, closed the door softly, stopped for a second and tossed the crumpled menu in a garbage can. And walked up the stairs to his apartment.

Acknowledgements

Thanks to my parents, Daphne and Keith, for the lifetime of love and support. Thanks to Jason and Jessica, and their families, for believing in me and having my back. Thanks to the great friends through the years who've never doubted I could put finger to keyboard, especially Pryor, Ethan, and Allison S.

Thanks to Julia for offering tons of great advice and for always being willing to read my very rough drafts.

Thanks to the many teachers, professors, and colleagues I've met along the way at Hopkinsville High School, the University of Louisville and the Department of Communication, Indiana University School of Journalism, the *Herald*, the CJ, Mental Floss, and elsewhere. Thanks also to those in the writing community in Louisville and southern Indiana I've come across.

To my wife, Megan, you've always believed in me and let me pursue my dreams. I'll always love you. To my kids, Ellison and Evia, you're too cool.

About the Author

An award-winning writer, Benjamin Lampkin has written for the *Herald* in Jasper, IN, the Louisville *Courier-Journal*, MentalFloss.com, Considerable.com, and the wellness app Okay Inside. He has also published short fiction in *LEO Weekly*. He lives in southern Indiana with his wife and two kids.

Made in the USA
Monee, IL
22 October 2021